I0546124

Poetry of an Addict:
Refined Reflections

Brett C. Persson

Poetry of an Addict:
Refined Reflections

All Rights Reserved

Second Printing

www.brettcpersson.com

@BrettCPersson

Cover Art and Illustrations

www.scpersson.art

www.nudouspublishing.com
info@nudouspublishing.com

Hardback ISBN: 978-1-964793-03-0
Paperback ISBN: 978-1-964793-02-3
Digital ISBN: 978-1-964793-01-6
Kindle ISBN: 978-1-964793-00-9

Dedication

To my loving family,

In the darkest hours, when shadows loomed large and the path forward seemed lost to the night, your unwavering light guided me back. Through the chaos of addiction, your love was the anchor in my storm, steadfast and unyielding. In every moment of despair, every second of doubt, you stood by me, your faith unbroken, your support unfaltering.

This journey, filled with trials and challenges, has been a testament to our strength together. Your patience, understanding, and unconditional love have been my salvation, a beacon of hope in the relentless darkness. You believed in me when I struggled to believe in myself, lifted me when I fell, and cheered for me with every step in my recovery.

Thank you for being my light in the darkness, strength in weakness, and hope in despair. This is not just my journey; it is ours.

7/26/24

Dear readers,

It was late at night in 1986, and my parents were in bed, and my brother was out. I got up from my Apple IIe to take a break or get inspiration for a D&D-style book I was trying to write called Deceit.

I opened my comic book box and took out my pint of Bacardi 151. I mixed it with some generic diet soda, and soon, I had a buzz. I had a heavy buzz after being stuck on what my hero should do after escaping the inn. That is when I had the idea to write poetry.

As my addiction to drugs and alcohol grew, I continued to write poetry. Then I went to detox and got clean, and I had an epiphany. I was going to publish my book of poetry. My profound and most excellent drug and alcohol-induced poetry. I mean, it was epic stuff, right?

That is how I came to release "Poetry of an Addict." Some of the poems were not bad, but most were. I thought if it rhymed, it was poetry, and I guess on some fundamental level, maybe it is.

Over the years, I have written several haiku books, which I feel are much better than my other poetry. I stopped writing poetry over a year ago to concentrate on writing novels and developing my writing skills. These awful adolescent poems out there kept nagging at me; they were unfinished.

The following is a remastering of some of those poems. I won't go as far as to call them works of art, but I do believe they are better. They are easier to read, have much better rhythm and meter, and they still rhyme. Whether they are good or bad, I can feel comfortable that they are better than they were, and I can stop being bothered by them and move on.

These poems may not be to everyone's taste, but they represent progress—a step forward in my writing journey. With this release, I can finally put aside the nagging sense of incompleteness and forge ahead.

Thank you for accompanying me on this journey. I hope you find solace or enjoyment in these pages; I know I have.

Warm regards,

Brett C. Persson

Table of Contents

Poetry of an Addict:
Refined Reflections

Part One

1

As Dawn's First Light Does Break,
My Demons Now Held In Their Wake.

Though My Mind Is Free,
Fear Still Lingers Within Me.

The Path Ahead Unclear,
But My Roots, I Hold Dear.

From Shadows, I've Broken Free,
Now Filled With Hope, You See.

Ready To Face The Fight,
Embracing Dawn's Bright Light.

2

Strolling Through The Park's Embrace,

In The Dark, Our Steps Find Grace.

Beneath The Night's Expansive View,

Stars Aglow, Casting Light Anew.

The Air's Caress, Gentle And Fair,

Hand In Hand, A Perfect Pair.

Around The Block, Our Bond Is Secure,

Fingers Entwined, Our Love Pure.

She, My Life's Sweet Song,

Forever By My Side, Lifelong.

In Our Union, Love's Decree,

Eternally, Together, We'll Be.

3

Witness His Fall,

Hear His Desperate Call.

See The Firearm's Glare,

Watch Him Flee In Despair.

To Evade The Fray,

Survival's The Only Way.

Hear The Hammer's Strike,

Surrender Seems Alike.

Hear The Gunshot's Cry,

Intensity Soaring High.

Crimson Streams Start To Flow,

No Escape, No Place To Go.

4

In The Grave, I Lay,

For Valor Led The Way.

Shot In The Chest, Alas,

In Noble Duty, Time Did Pass.

My Heart Quickens Its Pace,

Confronting Fate, I Embrace.

A Gaze Meets Mine, A Trace,

In That Moment, Time And Space.

5

In My Future, A Bleak Sight,

Shotgun Pressed, An Endless Night.

Sweat Beads, Fear's Call,

Hammer Strikes, Fate's Thrall.

Now Filled With Lead,

Blood Runs Red, Life Bled.

For Lost Love, Beth's Name,

I End The Game, My Own Claim.

6

In Love With A Girl, Fair As A Pearl,

At First, Our Romance Did Swirl.

Moments Sweet, With Joy Immersed,

Yet Swiftly Came The Bubble's Burst.

My Heart She Tore When We Did Part,

Leaving Me With A Shattered Heart.

Now I See, Clear As Day,

Love's Illusions Can Decay.

Once She Held My Everything,

Now Her Absence, An Echoing Sting.

I Miss Her Now, And Always Will,

Her Absence A Void, Time Cannot Fill.

I Paid The Toll, Forlorn And Cold,

As She Took My Soul, A Story Untold.

Without Love's Light, Life's Hues Are Dim,

A Barren Landscape, A Soulless Hymn.

7

Cheers Resound, Beers In Hand,

Smoke Swirls, Jokes Expand.

Wine Flows, Feeling Sublime,

But Too Much, Lost In Time.

Leaning Now, Jim Beam's Sway,

Pot Smoke Clouds, Minds Astray.

Seeking A Mate As The Night Unfurls,

But Time Slips Away In Alcohol's Swirls.

Time To Depart, Alcohol's Grip Tight,

Foe Revealed In The Sobering Light.

Caught In The Web Of A DUI,

Too Much Rye, A Costly High.

8

At The Bar, Drinks Flow Free,

But Then It's Time To Flee.

A Bowl Is Smoked, But Then A Toll,

As The Car Veers Out Of Control.

Limbs Fail, Speech Is Lost,

Intoxication's Heavy Cost.

Behind The Wheel, Impaired Senses Steal,

Unable To Grasp What's Real.

9

Once Revered, Now Just A Rag,

The American Flag Begins To Sag.

Pride Lost, To The Other Side,

Into Prisons, We Did Abide.

Their Flag Ascends, Ours Forgotten,

Careless, We Let Our Pride Be Rotten.

Indifference Reigns, We Hardly Care,

As The Bear Emerges, Our Spirit Wear.

With Nothing Left To Stir Our Roar,

The Eagle's Spirit Fades, Nevermore.

10

I Feel A Chill In The Air,

A Shadow Lingering There.

A Sense Of Something Wrong,

I've Felt It For So Long.

I Dare Not Make A Noise,

Afraid I'll Lose My Poise.

I Hope It Fades Away,

And Doesn't Plan To Stay.

I Fcel His Presence Near,

God, Please Take My Fear.

Who Is This Stranger Here,

Who Fills My Heart With Fear?

His Touch Is Cold And Cruel,

Unnatural, Like A Ghoul.

11

I Held The Gun, A Deadly Choice,

In His Bed, Silence's Voice.

Shot Her Dead, The Deed Complete,

What's Right, What's Wrong, In Defeat.

The Sight Of Blood, A Chilling Need,

Vengeance Claimed, A Ruthless Deed.

With Gun In Hand, The Act Is Spun,

Vengeance Claimed, The Damage Done.

12

I Hit The Shard With All My Might,

Crystal Clouds, A Hazy Sight.

Smoke Curls, I Take A Toke,

Fast Feelings, Past Evoked.

Releasing A Sigh, Weightless Flight,

Soaring High In The Dead Of Night.

Pipe Slips From My Grasp, Unplanned,

Life Feels Grand In This Distant Land.

With Newfound Drive, I Strive To Thrive,

Feeling Alive, I'll Surely Survive.

13

Standing Tall, On The Ledge I Stand,

Ready To Flee, Escape Life's Demand.

Peering Down, The City Below,

A Choice To Make, To Stay Or Go.

Yes Or No, A Final Plea,

Should I Jump And Be Set Free?

What Life Have I Known, How Deep The Bleed,

Counting The Scars, Of Desperate Need.

Voices Echo, Their Calls Resound,

Society's Sickness, Tightly Wound.

Watch Me Leap Into The Sky,

Listen Closely As I Say Goodbye.

14

Take His Life With Your Knife, Cold And Keen,
Avenge Your Son, Make Him Scream.

Stab The Bastard, Let Vengeance Flow,
In Your Rage, Let Justice Show.

He Took Your Child, Your Flesh And Blood,
Now It's His Turn, Let The Vengeance Flood.

With Each Strike, Feel The Anger Rise,
Tears Mix With Blood, Vengeance In Your Eyes.

No Mercy For The Man Who Stole Your Joy,
Each Wound Inflicted, Revenge Employ.

But As The Deed Is Done, And The Man Lies Still,
Will It Bring Solace, Will It Fulfill?

For Vengeance Taken May Ease The Pain,

Yet Emptiness Remains, A Haunting Stain.

So As You Stand There, Bloodied Knife In Hand,

Will Peace Return To This Grief-Stricken Land?

Or Will Vengeance Only Breed More Hate,

As The Cycle Of Violence Claims Its State?

In The End, What Will You Find,

When Vengeance Leaves Its Mark Behind?

15

I Hear The War Drums Beat,

Echoing Death On Every Street.

Children Fall, Their Laughter Stilled,

In The Crossfire Of Hate, Innocence Killed.

Echoes Of Violence, A Relentless Roar,

Claiming The Lives Of The Impoverished And More.

Beneath The Rubble, Voices Wail,

As Hope Dwindles, And Dreams Turn Pale.

I Hear The Anguished Cries,

As Families Say Their Last Goodbyes.

Families Torn Asunder, Their Cries Pierce The Sky,

As They Bid Farewell To Loved Ones, Unable To Defy

In The Midst Of Chaos And Despair,

Will Humanity's Conscience Dare?

To Halt The Violence, To Seek Peace,

And From This Cycle Of Death, Release.

For In The Sound Of War's Cruel Song,

Lies The Plea For Righting Wrong.

So Let Us Listen, Let Us Hear,

The Call For Peace, Ringing Clear.

To Build A Future Where Violence Dies,

And In Its Place, Hope And Love Arise.

16

Behold This Space, Its Beauty's Grace,

Yet Race Consumes, A Bitter Chase.

Peer Within, Let Your True Self Show,

No Need To Hide, Let Your Spirit Grow.

Be Who You Are, Embrace Your Will,

No Need For Violence, No One To Kill.

Color's A Veneer, Skin-Deep It Creeps,

What You Sow, A Harvest Reaps.

So Be Kind In Every Mind,

For Death Knows Not Color, To All It's Blind.

17

Doubt Creeps In As Lights Fade Away,

Mac In Hand, To End The Fray.

You Draw Your Mac, A Lethal Pact,

To End Their Track, A Ruthless Act.

But Too Late, Fate's Die Is Cast,

Trigger Pulled, Time Flies Fast.

Who Would Have Thought, This Grim Picture,

Death's Harvest, An Unexpected Fixture.

All Slain, The Burden Falls,

For Such A Mass, Justice Calls.

Gas Chamber Waits, Its Chilling Grasp,

For One Who Dared, Life's Final Gasp.

18

In The Shadows, He Roams Alone,

A Soul Adrift, A Heart Of Stone.

Haunted By Demons, Unseen And Real,

Lost In A Cycle He Can't Conceal.

Each Sip A Balm, A Fleeting Relief,

But Deeper He Falls, In His Own Grief.

Chasing Away The Ghosts Of The Past,

But The Darkness Within, It Holds Him Fast.

The Bottle, His Only Companion At Night,

In Its Embrace, He Seeks Respite.

Yet The More He Drinks, The Deeper He Sinks,

Into The Abyss, Where Despair Blinks.

Days Blend Into Nights, And Nights Into Days,

Lost In A Haze, In A Timeless Daze.

He Longs For Escape, For A Glimmer Of Light,

To Break Free From The Chains That Bind Him Tight.

In The Depths Of Despair, He Finds No Reprieve,

As Darkness Consumes, No Chance To Retrieve.

Lost In A Cycle, Where Shadows Grow,

His Spirit Withers, His Will Brought Low.

Yet Hope Flickers Still, In The Depths Of His Heart,

A Tiny Ember, Refusing To Depart.

Yearning For Freedom, From This Endless Plight,

That Even In Darkness, There Can Be Light.

19

It Burns As It Enters, I Know It's A Sin,

But It Feels So Right, A Battle Within.

My Throat Tightens, Craving's Might,

Can't Go Without, In The Dead Of Night.

Easy To Begin, Hard To Depart,

Addiction's Grip, A Tightening Heart.

I Know I'm Sick, But It's A Cunning Deceit,

Once We Fought, Now Thoughts Retreat.

Resistance Fades, Lost In Its Clutch,

Disconnected Now, From Reality's Touch.

20

Mind Starts To Wander, Lost In The Thunder,

As You Ponder The Fate That Tore You Asunder.

Snatched By A Gun In The Still Of The Night,

Before The Dawn, Before Morning Light.

The Trigger Pulled By A Thug's Reckless Hand,

Leaving Your World In A Shattered Land.

A Life Once Filled With Love, Now Shattered And Torn,

In The Depths Of Grief, You're Left To Mourn.

No Reason, No Rhyme, Just Senseless Pain,

In The Aftermath Of Loss, Only Tears Remain.

Your Soul Pierced By The Thorn Of Grief,

Every Heartbeat, A Silent Thief.

No Reason, No Rhyme, Just Senseless Pain,

Your World Forever Altered, Never The Same.

Part Two

21

A Clarity Profound,

Rare Treasure Found.

Above The Clouds I Soar,

Strength To The Core.

Rolling Waves Of Thought,

Kindness Sought.

All-Knowing, They Say,

Drugs Beckon, Lead The Way.

Chew And Consume,

Youthful, In The Bloom.

Blissful Highs It Brings,

Believing I Have Wings.

22

Flowing, It Starts, No Bounds To Know,
No Depths Too Low To Bestow.

Mind Racing In Its Own Embrace,
Let Me Present My Case.

Drugs, They Unlock, Expand The Mind,
Discoveries, Treasures To Find.

Grand Feelings Surge, As The Band Plays,
Strong Sensations In Vibrant Arrays.

Nothing's Amiss, All Feels So Right,
Come Join, Revel In The Night.

Watch As I Grin, Wide And Free,
In This Moment, Just Let Me Be.

23

In This Lonely Chair I Dwell,

Life's Cruel Toll I Know Too Well.

Sip By Sip, The Shadows Grow,

As Life's Bitter Currents Flow.

Bottles Strewn Upon The Floor,

Echoes Of A Love No More.

Dreams Of Her, A Distant Cheer,

Yet I Clutch My Faithful Beer.

Whispers Of A Time Long Past,

Moments Fleeting, Never Last.

Silent Tears And Silent Cries,

Hope Diminished, Sorrowed Skies.

Wanting, To Feel Her Near,

But Solace Lies Within My Tear.

In This Elegy, I Pour,

Heartache's Dirge Forevermore.

24

Sunday's Light, I Rise From Sleep,
Seeking Respite, My Soul To Keep.

My Body Aches, Each Movement Sore,
Tasks Feel Heavy, A Tiresome Chore.

Memories Linger From The Night,
A Mixture Of Thrill And Slight Fright.

Reflections Of My Life's Past Deeds,
Stirring Inner Turmoil, It Feeds.

I Seek Relief, From Pain's Cruel Lore,
To Keep It At Bay, Off Distant Shore.

In Life's Crossroads, I Must Endure,
Through Trials Faced, I Seek A Cure.

Lost Within The Bar's Dim Light,
I Soar Like A Star, Burning Bright.

Yet Soon I Fear, My Light May Fade,

Doubts Cast Shadows, A Masquerade.

Trapped Within This Bottle's Hold,

Life's Throttle, A Story Told.

25

Desiring An End, But The Fun's Allure,

Seeking Cleanliness, Yet Drawn To Impure.

Longing For Calm, Amidst This Din,

In The Grasp Of Drugs, I Constantly Spin.

Yearning For Clarity, But Charity I Seek,

Alone In My Battles, No Friend To Speak.

Regretting My Choices, Strayed From The Path,

Lost In The Tempest, Facing Its Wrath.

Dreaming Of Freedom From This Endless Chase,

But Bound By Addiction, A Prisoner's Embrace.

Hoping For Change, Yet Stuck In My Ways,

In This Endless Cycle, My Spirit Sways.

Wishing For Love To Break Through The Night,

But Instead, I Find Solace In The Flight.

Craving Relief From This Consuming Curse,

Yet Holding Onto The Drugs, For Better Or Worse.

Longing For Strength To Break From This Chain,

But The Grip Tightens, Causing More Pain.

Seeking Redemption, A Chance To Revive,

But Drowning In Shadows, Unable To Thrive.

Searching For Solace, But Met With Disdain,

In This Lonely Journey, My Efforts In Vain.

Yearning For Healing, Yet Still Drawn Astray,

In The Darkness, My Soul Starts To Fray.

Seeking Salvation From This Relentless Plight,

But The Drugs Hold Me Fast, Despite The Fight.

Praying For Guidance, A Light In The Dark,

But My Pleas Go Unanswered, Lost In The Spark.

Hoping For Change, In This Endless War,

But Trapped In The Turmoil, Forevermore.

Wishing For Peace, In This Tumultuous Ride,

But The Storm Rages On, With Nowhere To Hide.

Longing For An End To This Painful Decree,

But In The Depths Of Despair, I Cannot Break Free.

Wishing For Mercy, In This Ceaseless Storm,

But In The Chaos, My Spirit Forlorn.

Desiring Reprieve, From This Constant Toll,

But In The Depths Of Addiction, I've Lost Control.

Longing Just To Exist,

But Life Demands A Fee, Persist.

Yearning To Thaw This Heart Grown Cold,

Yet Age Claims Its Grip, Bold.

Desiring To Quit This Endless Trap,

But Drugs Allure, A Relentless Rap.

Craving To Feel, To Break This Numb,

Yet Emptiness Echoes, Deaf And Dumb.

Wishing For Talent To Draw, Create,

But Fate Dealt A Hand, Sealed My Fate.

Dreaming Of Purpose, A Calling True,

But Struggles Feel More Like A Rue.

Seeking Balance, To Walk A Steady Line,

Yet In Shadows, I'm Unable To Shine.

Yearning To Sail, To Venture, To Roam,

Yet Adrift, I Merely Drift, Alone.

Longing To Strive, To Push, To Dare,

But Coasting, I Find, Leaves Me Bare.

Wishing To Be A Beacon, A Guide,

Yet Lost In The Darkness, I Abide.

Seeking Comprehension, To Be Seen,

Yet In My Chaos, I Remain Unseen.

Desiring To Make A Mark, Leave A Trace,

Yet Reverence Eludes, In This Space.

Hoping For Guidance, A Path To Heed,

Yet In Uncertainty, I Plant No Seed.

Wishing For Peace, In A Tumultuous Race,

Yet Turmoil Engulfs, Leaving No Space.

Longing For Fairness, A Chance To Redeem,

Yet Fear's Grip Tightens, A Chilling Scream.

Yearning For Learning, To Grow And Mend,

Yet Lessons Unlearned, Still I Descend.

Seeking Solace For Those I Hold Dear,

Yet The Toll Of Life Whispers Fear.

Dreaming Of Luck, A Fortunate Hand,

Yet The Game's End Nears, No Strand.

Longing To Escape The Burden Of Guilt,

Yet Wounds Reopen, Where Pain Was Built.

Desiring Freedom From A Past's Grip,

Yet Haunted By Memories, I Slip.

Wishing For Sustenance, To Nourish The Soul,

Yet Rudeness Masks, A Heart's Toll.

Seeking Shelter, A Place To Stay,

Yet Turned Away, Where Shadows Play.

Dreaming Of Being Chosen, Valued, Seen,

Yet Overlooked, In A World So Keen.

Hoping For Recognition, A Name To Claim,

Yet Overlooked, In This Familial Game.

Longing To Return To A Childhood Abode,

Yet Past Mistakes, A Heavy Load.

Yearning For Solace In A Bottle's Cheer,

Yet The Void Remains, In Silence, Austere.

Longing To Depart From This Stagnant Bay,

Yet Rooted In Place, I Must Stay.

Desiring To Spread Life's Seed,

Yet Barren Ground, Where Hearts Bleed.

Seeking Solace In Prayer's Embrace,

Yet Only Playfulness Finds Its Place.

26

Waking On The Wrong Side, Her Eyes Agape,

A Violent Slap, The Room's Still Shape.

Screams Echo, A Vicious Sound,

Tension Thick, Chaos Unbound.

She Draws A Gun, Fun's Demise,

Her Hand Steady, No Disguise.

With A Click, The Slide's Retracted,

In The Air, Tension Refracted.

The Bullet Pierces, Skin To Bone,

Silence Falls, No Words Intone.

You Collapse, Life's Thread Unwed,

Tears Fall, For The Life That's Bled.

27

Took Her Son, Armed Him For The Fight,

Sent Him Off, To Darkness And Light.

In The Heat Of War, Hear His Cry,

Fierce And Bold, Beneath The Sky.

Became A Hero, Stood The Test,

But Fell To Bullets, In His Chest.

Fought For What's Right, With All His Might,

Dreaming Of Home, In The Quiet Night.

His Mother's Sorrow, Heavy As The Sea,

Scatters His Ashes, Where Waves Break Free.

28

Lost In The Grip Of Meth's Embrace,
Unfazed By Death, In Its Chase.

Riding The High To Ease The Pain,
Using It As A Crutch, In Vain.

Letting Your Spirit Ascend,
For This, Meth Is A Friend.

Feeling The Calm It Bestows,
In Its Pleasure, The Soul Grows.

Fueled By A Surge Of Might,
As If Soaring To A Towering Height.

Senses Heightened, In Tune,
Gazing At The Moon.

Wondering What Lies Beyond,
Fierce As A Bear, Yet Fond.

Sometimes Consumed By Rage,

Confined Within A Mental Cage.

Losing Grasp, Spiraling Down,

Dancing To The Tune Of Parole's Crown.

Eyes Darting, Wary Of The Law,

Disregarding Authority's Claw.

Thriving On The Adrenaline Rush,

Shaking Off The Cold's Hush.

Lost In The Maze Of Your Mind,

No Solace There To Find.

29

Open The Door, Glide Upon The Floor,

Tilt The Bottle Back, Sobriety's Door.

Feeling The Heat, As The Liquid Meets,

Mind Starts To Wander, To Familiar Streets.

To A Place Well-Known, Where Troubles Have Flown,

Vision Blurs, But Certainty's Grown.

Care Falls Away, In This Realm You Stay,

Lost In The Moment, Lost In The Fray.

You're In That Space, Setting Your Own Pace,

As Darkness Encroaches, In This Race.

Drifting To Black, No Turning Back,

In This Oblivion, Reality Slack.

Forget The Bash, Soon To Crash,

Wake To The Morning's Harsh Lash.

The Ritual Begins, Habitual Sins,

Can't Break The Cycle, Where Darkness Grins.

Can't Stay Straight, Bottle Is Your Fate,

Trapped In This Cycle, Bound By Weight.

30

Drenched In Darkness, In The Park's Embrace,

Starting To See The Shadows Of My Own Face.

Soul Turned Black, Devoid Of Grace,

When God Tore Us Apart, Leaving No Trace.

Lost My Reason, My Beloved Wife,

Now Left With Nothing, But Pain And Strife.

She Was Everything, Better Than The Rest,

Her Presence Filled Me, Made Me My Best.

Happy In Union, Now I'm A Ghost,

Her Absence Haunting, My Soul Engrossed.

I Ache For Her, Why Did She Depart?

Wanting To End It All, Consumed By Heart.

Gun To My Temple, Blood To Be Bled,

To Reunite With Her, Or So It's Said.

Terrified To Let Go, Yet I Must Try,

Desperate To Escape This Endless Cry.

Fear Of God's Judgment, As I Teeter On The Brink,

But The Longing For I Dare Not To Even Blink.

She Was My Ally, Yet I Couldn't Defend,

Left Defenseless, As Her Life Met Its End.

Her Assailant Roams Free, No Justice In Sight,

Anguish Fuels My Resolve, To Make It Right.

As I Pull The Trigger, Under The Moon's Soft Light,

I Hope To Join Her Soon, In The Eternal Night.

31

I Stumble And I Fall,

Trapped Within These Walls.

My Life Seeps Away,

Left Here To Decay.

No One Hears A Sound,

I Will Not Be Found.

Silent Shadows Creep,

As I Sink Into Sleep.

My Cries Go Unheard,

Lost Like A Fallen Bird.

In Darkness, I Remain,

Bound By Endless Pain.

32

The Love Of Your Wife, A Cherished Part,

Enriches Life, A Work Of Art.

Hold Her Close, Her Tender Face,

She Fits So Right, In Life's Embrace.

In Her Presence, Your World's In Tune,

Kindness Spreads Beneath The Moon.

Guided By Fate, Led By Divine,

In Her Arms, True Love Entwined.

Her Acceptance, A Precious Gleam,

Your Shared Bond, A Cherished Dream.

Best Friend And Partner, Hand In Hand,

Together Through Life's Shifting Sand.

33

God Within, My Heart's True Start,

His Love, A Flame, Off The Chart.

Belief Ignites Life's Vibrant Flame,

In Giving, Find Our Truest Aim.

Extend A Hand To Sisters, Brothers,

Uplift Them, Share With Others.

In Christ's Embrace, I Find My Song,

Secure In Where I Belong.

Though Doubts May Cloud, Faith's Light Persists,

In Him, Our Strength, Our Souls Resist.

He Stands Beside Through Every Tide,

In Him, Our Fears, We Confide.

When Trials Loom And Skies Turn Grey,

He Bears Us Through, Come What May.

In His Embrace, We Find Our Place,

Guided By His Boundless Grace.

Through Trials Faced, In Every Space,

He Helps Us Run Life's Steady Race.

Beside You, He'll Firmly Abide,

Through Life's Tumultuous Ride.

When Strength Falters, And Doubts Accrue,

His Grace Uplifts, Sees You Through.

In His Embrace, Find Solace Deep,

His Love, A Comfort In Times Of Sleep.

Endless, Boundless, His Love Extends,

Mending Hearts, And Pain It Mends.

34

Upon The Cross, He Hangs In Pain,

Mocked And Scorned, Amidst Disdain.

A Spear Is Thrust, His Side They Pierce,

Their Fear And Hate, His Love To Fierce.

For Our Sins, He Bears The Weight,

Yet Victory Is His Final Fate.

His Teachings Spread, His Love Ablaze,

Three Days Hence, His Power Displays.

From Death's Embrace, He Does Arise,

Thorns Once Worn, Now Shattered Lies.

Salvation's Gift, He Freely Bestows,

From Damnation's Grasp, He Shields And Knows.

35

Grace Of God, A Radiant Crown,

Illuminating The Town.

Spreading Wide His Boundless Grace,

Enveloping Every Place.

Ever-Watchful, Guiding Hand,

Keeping Us From Shifting Sand.

In Our Need, He's Ever Near,

In Word And Deed, His Love Sincere.

Hope He Grants In Times Of Woe,

Teaching Us The Way To Grow.

In His Arms, We Find Our Peace,

Amidst Life's Storms, His Love Won't Cease.

When Darkness Fades, And Shadows Flee,

In His Light, All Will Be Free.

36

Hard To Speak Of What I Feel Inside,

Struggling To Keep The Truth And Lies Untied.

You Turn Away, Not Wanting To Hear,

The Whispers Of My Deepest Fear.

You Sought A Perfect Child, Bright And Grand,

But Fate Dealt A Different Hand.

In Desperate Need, I Call For Aid,

Lost In The Troubles I've Made.

I'm Losing The Essence Of Who I Am,

My Soul's A Wanderer, On The Lam.

The End Seems Near, Not Far Away,

My Life Has Strayed, Gone Astray.

I Wish I Could Have Brought You Pride,

Both You And Father, Side By Side.

But Now, The Time Has Come For Me To Part,

I Hope This Journey Does Not Break Your Heart.

May It Be Swift, My Final Breath,

A Peaceful Passage Into Death.

37

Wrapped Up Tight In Bed You Lay,

A Cold In Your Head, Clouds Your Day.

Feeling Down And Out, Like Total Shit,

Your Fever's Flame, Won't Seem To Quit.

This Ailment Grips, Relentless Feeling,

Your Body Reels, In Fever's Reeling.

Longing For Health, Each Moment Tougher,

Brow Damp With Sweat, The Fever's Buffer.

Hoping For Dawn To Break The Gloom,

To Lift This Shroud Of Illness' Doom.

Tired Of This Plight, Feeling Sick,

Like A Warrior, Ready To Kick.

38

I Hear Your Words, But I'm Not Staying,
Get It For Me, Or Let Me Be Swaying.

How About Some Blow, The Urge Is Strong,
Quick, Before My Will Is Gone.

Just An Eight Ball, Before I Hit The Floor,
I Need It Bad, Can't Take It Anymore.

Back To My Pad, It's Where I'll Be,
Fuel My Need, Set My Soul Free.

I Am In Need, My Craving Dire,
My Nose To Feed, My Desire On Fire.

I Wake, Craving Coke, With Dawn's First Light,
Waiting On It, My Mood Takes Flight.

As You Can Guess, I Am A Mess, Tangled In Distress,
Cocaine's Grasp, Relentless Duress.

39

I Spot The Car, Sitting In The Dark,

Windows Tinted Dark, Near The Park.

Waiting For The Right Time To Drop The Dime,

Watching My Every Move, In This Tense Mime.

Observing All I Do, Oh, So True,

He Aims To End Me, It's Overdue.

I Crossed Someone's Way, Now I Must Pay,

I Could Try And Run, But I Know It's Nay.

His Grip Tightens, Soon I'll Be Done,

Paying The Price For The Deeds I've Spun.

His Victory Nears, My End Draws Near,

For My Sins, I'll Face The Final Frontier.

40

Read My Lips, Feel My Sway,

In The Shadows Where Passions Play.

Dim The Light, Ignite The Night,

Make Every Touch Feel Just Right.

Embrace The Thrill, Let It Be Rough,

In The Heat Of Love, We're Bold Enough.

Passion Ignites, A Blazing Pyre,

In This Union, Our Souls Aspire.

Part Three

41

I See A Wasteland, Stretches Of Sand,

Once Lush And Green, Now Barren Land.

Trees, Now Gone, No Brush In Sight,

And Where Lawns Flourished, Only Blight.

Buildings, Now Rubble, Lay On The Floor,

Devastation Reigns, From A War's Fierce Roar.

No Souls In Sight, All Disappeared,

Silent Echoes, What Once Was Revered.

42

I Visit My Shrink, Teetering On The Brink,

He Knows Me Well, My Thoughts He Can Link.

Feeling So Sad, Never A Glint Of Glad,

Always Dwelling On The Worst, My Happiness A Tad.

Putting Others First, I'm Left Feeling Crappy,

While He Listens, I Confide, Never Feeling Sappy.

He Offers His Aid, This Much I Concede,

Lending Me An Ear, As I Express My Need.

43

He Steps Into His Car, Ready To Roam,

Driving Far, Seeking Places Unknown.

Off On Vacation, Across The Nation's Sweep,

A Journey To Take, Where Memories Will Keep.

Venturing On A Small Trip, To Where Vibes Are Hip,

Meeting New Faces, With A Smile And A Quip.

No Plans In Hand, Just Him And His Wheels,

Exploring Freely, Wherever The Road Reveals.

44

I Gifted You Candy, Oh So Dandy,

With Wine To Dine, Our Evening Planned.

A Charm I Sought, A Harmless Charm Bought,

A Cat To Grace, But It Stayed In Place.

Lunch I Provided, A Hunch It Might Be One-Sided,

A Car I Secured, Not Quite What You Preferred.

A Ring In Hand, But Your Silence I Couldn't Stand,

So Much I Bought, Your Touch Now Naught.

Gold I Bestowed, Yet You Remained Cold,

A Couch To Share, But You Found Despair.

A House We Own, Yet I'm Alone,

Called A Louse, In Our Once-Shared House.

45

Numbness Overtakes My Feet,

Post-Drug Treat, A Fleeting Meet.

Washed It Down With Crimson Wine,

Feeling Fine, In A Haze Divine.

Mind Adrift, Lost And Found,

In This Surreal Playground.

Next Week Beckons, A Familiar Call,

Turning Into A Thrill-Seeking Thrall.

There's So Much More To Explore.

Why Didn't I Tread This Path Before?

Yearning To Find That Elusive Tune,

Eyes Wide As The Glowing Moon.

46

Onward, To The Scene

With Eyes So Keen

Swerving Lanes, So Bold

Madness Untold

With A Drunk At The Wheel

Reckless Appeal

Fateful Choice, A Sin

Life Spins, A Spin

Tree's Embrace, So Cold

No Escape Foretold

Through Glass, You Yield

In A Field, Revealed

In A Heap, You Lie

Face Kissed By Sky

Blood Stains The Earth

In The Grasp Of Death's Mirth

Closer, The Reaper's Sight

Fear Takes Its Flight

Mother's Tears, They'll Flow

As You Lay Low

Peace Eludes, Profound

In Soil, You're Bound

Her Heart, It Breaks So

A Simple No Could Bestow

47

Behold Mr. Dunn,

Quick On The Run.

Pursuing Mr. Glass,

For Justice, He'll Amass.

Now Within His Sight,

In The Fray Of What's Right.

Swiftly Must He Act,

To Prevent More Impact.

Elijah, To The Cell,

Justice's Call Must Quell.

Once Escaped, He's Cunning,

But Dunn's Resolve Is Stunning.

48

In My Leather Chair,

Life's Weight I Bear.

My Chest Constricts, Tight,

An Internal Fight.

Pain Shoots Through My Arm,

Sounding The Alarm.

Feeling Ill, So Quick,

Death's Shadow, So Thick.

Heart In Arrest, My Plight,

Ignoring Signs Wasn't Right.

Delaying Tests, My Error,

Ignored The Warning Bearer.

At Thirty-Three, Life's Decree,

Remember Me, Fondly.

49

My Beeper's Beep, A Note To Heed,

Time Now To Collect My Fee Indeed.

Gotta Grab That Cash, No Time To Thrash,

Just A Quick Dash, No Time To Clash.

In The Game Of Drugs, I Claim My Fame,

Every Soul Knows My Name's Acclaim.

From Big To Small, I Fulfill Them All,

Your Needs, I Heed, Your Cravings Fall.

In The Trade Of Drugs, I Reign Supreme,

My Name Echoes In Every Dream.

They Never Let Me Be, Always On The Spree,

Working Deals, Where Wounds Find Their Plea.

Ensuring I've Enough, Though Times Get Rough,

For Business Thrives When Stocks Are Enough.

My Turf's My Hood, Where Business Brews,

Go Elsewhere? They'd Refuse, They'd Lose.

50

Imprisoned Here, My Lonely Cell,

A Silent Witness To My Fall,

Where Shadows Of My Choices Dwell,

And Echoes Of My Guilt Enthrall.

In Chains Of Sorrow, I Am Bound,

For Sins That Built This Life Of Pain,

In Silence, Hear The Mournful Sound,

Of Dreams Now Lost, In Dark Refrain.

Once Ablaze With Passion's Fire,

Now Cold, I Face My Destined Lot,

From Heights Of Hope To Depths So Dire,

In This Forsaken Cell, I Rot.

51

In The Night's Embrace, Whispers In The Air,

Beyond The Veil, Mysteries To Share.

Streets Pulse With Life, Where Shadows Dance,

In Their Rhythm, I Find My Chance.

A Tapestry Of Tales, Woven In The Night,

In Every Corner, A New Delight.

A Symphony Of Souls, In Varied Hues,

Each Step I Take, A Different Muse.

With Each Passing Hour, The City's Heartbeat,

In Its Rhythm, My Essence Sweet.

Through The Night's Expanse, I Take Flight,

Guided By Stars, In The Velvet Night.

52

Another Officer Falls, Duty's Weight He Bore,

A Villain's Bullet Strikes, Tragedy's Score.

She Upheld The Law, With Courage Ripe,

As Criminals Conspired, In Shadows To Swipe.

But One Dark Soul Met, A Fate Well Earned,

His Cowardice Resounded, As His Body Turned.

Now We Mourn, The Loss So Deep,

For A Hero's Life, We Silently Weep.

Her Father's Heart, Now Heavy With Grief,

As Memories Haunt, Without Relief.

Oh, If Only She Could Grace Us Here,

Instead, Her Valor's Tale, We Sadly Revere.

In Gear Of Duty, She Found Her End,

A Life Cut Short, A Heart To Mend.

53

In The Depths Where I Languished, Sinking Low,

I Sought Solace In Liquor's Amber Flow.

Beer, My Faithful Companion, Through Nights Drear,

Shielding Me From The Shadows Of My Fear.

Love's Embrace I Shunned, From High Above,

Believing Solitude Was My Only Glove.

Alone In My Torment, No One To Confide,

In My Private Hell, I Chose To Abide.

Pushed Away My Wife, From My Heart's Core,

In Solitude, I Sought Solace More And More.

Living For The Drink, Life Teetering On The Brink,

A Cycle Unbroken, Or So I'd Think.

What More Can I Express, In This Somber Song,

Misguided For Too Long, My Path Was Wrong.

54

Oh, Your Beauty Divine, A Feast For My Eyes,

In Your Allure, My Admiration Lies.

A Vision Of Loveliness, My Thoughts Unfurl,

Your Grace And Charm, My Senses Whirl.

Captivated By Your Allure, Hooked Indeed,

In Your Presence, I Find All I Need.

You're My Perfect Counterpart, A Match So True,

Bound To You, My Love Ever Grew.

With You By My Side, I Soar To The Sky,

Your Presence Makes Every Goal Seem Nigh.

Supporting Me In Every Endeavor, It's True,

Because Of You, I Can Pursue.

In Times Of Distress, You're My Solace, My Rock,

In Your Embrace, I Weather Life's Knock.

Completing My Existence, As Husband And Wife,

With You, My Love, I Navigate Life.

55

In Ecstasy's Embrace, Feeling Sublime,
On X's Thrill, I Dance In Time.

Mind Whirls In A Fevered Race,
Each Moment A Thrill, A Pulsing Chase.

The Sensation, Surreal, Beyond Belief,
In Its Allure, I Find Sweet Relief.

Let It Sweep Me Away, Take Its Toll,
In Its Embrace, I Find My Soul.

Oh, The Rush Of Euphoria, I Extol,
Rolling In Ecstasy, Heart And Soul.

56

In God, Find Solace, Your Every Need,
His Nourishment For Your Soul, Indeed.

He'll Elevate Your Life, Make It Grand,
Rescue You From Satan's Cunning Hand.

Place Faith In The Lord, Your Shield And Guide,
Against The Evil Horde, He'll Abide.

Spread His Love, A Beacon From Above,
Feel His Grace, A Testament Of His Love.

He'll Ensure You Stand Firm, Never To Fall,
The Architect Of Creation, Over All.

His Love Knows No Bounds, Endless In Its Span,
Sent His Son, Jesus, For The Salvation Of Man.

Keep Him In Your Thoughts, His Presence Near,
Worship Him, And Tranquility Shall Appear.

When Life's Trials Assail, When Times Grow Rough,

He'll Carry You Through, Resilient And Tough.

Every Word You Utter, He Hears It Clear,

Listen To His Messages Of Hope, Don't Veer.

Shutting Him Out Due To Doubt, Don't Prolong,

Hear The Angels' Harmonious Song.

Gaze Upon His Countenance, Absorb His Grace,

In His Holy Book, Find Guidance, Find Your Place.

57

Strumming My Guitar, In The Local Dive,

Earning A Buck Or Two, To Keep Dreams Alive.

Playing Tunes Fresh, Something To Renew,

In Every Chord, A Piece Of Me I Imbue.

A Sound I've Crafted, Hoping It Will Spread,

Seeking That Break, Where My Own Path's Led.

I Revel In The Melody, In My Own Unique Sway,

For Music, My Passion, I Live It Every Day.

In Its Embrace, I Find My Liberation, My Key,

Music, Oh Music, It Means Everything To Me.

58

Through The Endless Night, I Stand, Prepared To Wage,

Seeking Out Trouble, With Each Passing Stage.

Downing Another Double, In The Dim-Lit Bar's Embrace,

Fueling The Rage Within, In This Shadowed Space.

The Distant Wail Of A Train, A Symphony Of Despair,

In Its Rhythmic Cadence, I Numb The Pain I Bear.

59

Should I Extend My Trust, Venture On A Limb,

Believe His Words, Despite The Grim?

He Claims He's Framed, His Honor At Stake,

Desperate To Evade The World's Cruel Rake.

Struggling To Uphold His Pristine Name,

To Shield His Legacy From Smears Of Shame.

Yearning For Clarity, To Cast Off Fear's Pall,

As The Specter Of Jail Looms Over All.

Accused Of A Heinous Deed, A Priest's Demise,

In The Media's Spotlight, His Reputation Fries.

He Leans On Me, His Chance To Flee The Dance Of Death,

His Salvation, Perhaps, In My Legal Breath.

Though His Reputation's Tarnished, His Name Maligned,

I'll Strive To Clear Him, Justice Defined.

In Pursuit Of The Truth, The Real Culprit To Reveal,

Lest They Hang Him From The Courthouse Seal.

Errors, I Must Eschew, Lest Justice Fail To Shine,

In This Battle For Truth, There's No Room For Decline.

Hope Dwindles As Time Slips Away,

To Absolve Him Of Guilt, I Must Lead The Way.

I Must Triumph In This Legal Race,

To Keep His Innocence, I Maintain The Pace.

Their Case, I Surmise, Lacks Firm Ground,

In This Courtroom Drama, Truth Will Be Found.

60

Invisible To Your Eyes, I Silently Plea,

Grant Me The Solace Of Being Free.

Weary Of Being A Pawn, A Mere Toy,

In The Hands Of A Thoughtless Boy.

All You Seek Is Pleasure, Fleeting And Base,

But I Refuse To Yield, To Be Part Of That Chase.

You Fail To Grasp The Depth Of My Worth,

Reducing Me To An Object For Mirth.

Part Four

61

To The Needy, I Open My Door,

In Giving, I Find My Soul's True Core.

If They Don't Grumble Or Whine,

Assistance I'm Ready To Define.

Sometimes It's Meals That I Provide,

When Compassion Flows Like A Tide.

Extending A Hand In Their Hour Of Need,

From Life's Quagmire, Helping Them To Be Freed.

Hoping They Find Their Footing Anew,

A Goal I Ardently Pursue.

Some Seek Aid To Clear A Debt,

Others Merely A Warm Shower To Get.

Many Wear Sadness Like A Shroud,

Bearing The Weight Of Life's Cloud.

But With Aid, A Spark Of Hope Ignites,

Guiding Them Through The Darkest Nights.

Slowly, Their Lives Begin To Mend,

As Prayers Find Their Destined End.

In Alleviating Their Pain And Strife,

I Play A Part In Rewriting Their Life.

Every Extra Mile, Every Deed,

Fuels The Warmth Of A Selfless Creed.

For Them, I Stand, I Advocate,

Fighting For What's Just, Never Abate.

62

Within My Mind, A Vision Forms Clear,

Of Those Behind Bars, Their Fate Severe.

Serving Out Their Time For Crimes They've Done,

Each Day Measured, Each Night Begun.

But My Vision Falters, It's Not So True,

Sentenced For Years, Yet Their Time's Askew.

Sentenced To Fifteen, A Span That's Grave,

Yet Overcrowded Cells, Their Freedom Crave.

Released In Far Less Than Their Rightful Decree,

Chaos Ensues, A System's Plea.

Let Not Justice Falter, Nor The System Flail,

Retain Them Securely, Behind Bars They'll Prevail.

63

I Revel In The High, Willing To Explore,

In The Realm Of Ecstasy, I Eagerly Soar.

A Sensation Sublime, Ascending To The Sky,

Drifting Like A Feather, As Time Slips By.

Oh, The Allure Of Drugs, A Flight Like A Dove,

In Their Embrace, I Discover Love.

They Grant Me Freedom, A Fleeting Reprieve,

With Each Hit, My Burdens I Leave.

A Brief Journey, A Temporary Stay,

In Altered States, I Find My Way.

An Exhilarating Ride, Unleashing My Wild Tide,

In Their Embrace, My Inhibitions Hide.

They Offer Solace, A Respite From Pain,

In Their Embrace, I Find My Sane.

64

Do You Ponder If He Exists, If He's Real?

What Emotions Within You Does It Unveil?

Could He Dwell Beyond The Clouds, Way Up High?

Dare To Believe, Or Dismiss With A Sigh?

Does He Offer Us Solace, A Beacon Of Hope?

Or Is It A Concept On Which Some Elope?

I Can't Claim To Know, It's A Mystery To Me,

Yet Some Assert With Certainty.

Their Conviction Resonates, Stirs Something Deep,

A Flicker Of Belief, From Its Slumber, Does Creep.

What If The Tales They Tell Are Indeed True?

What Path Should I Tread, What Steps Should I Pursue?

I Sense A Presence, A Force To Keep Me Alive,

Could It Be His Grace, Helping Me Thrive?

Should I Embrace His Guidance, Let It Shape My Way,

Or Turn Away, And Salvation Betray?

Hope That His Counsel Steers Me Just Right,

Guiding Me Through Darkness, Revealing The Light.

65

Tried A Sip Of DNA, Not Bad, I Confess,

A Fruity Concoction, Inviting, I Assess.

Kind Of Good, Its Flavor Enticing,

With Each Sip, The Urge For More Is Rising.

Guzzle It Down, Like A True Drinking Man,

In The Depths Of Intoxication, I Am A Fan.

Love To Get Lost In The Haze Of A Drink,

Inebriation's Embrace, It's Easier To Think.

No Destination In Sight, Nowhere To Be,

Just Wandering Aimlessly, Feeling Free.

Eager To Meet New Faces On The Street,

Under The Influence, Every Encounter's A Feat.

Alcohol, My Loyal Companion In The Night,

In Its Glow, My True Self Takes Flight.

Unveiling Aspects Hidden Deep Within,

A Revelation, A Journey To Begin.

Observing People As They Are, From Near Or Far,

Understanding Their Essence, Beneath Each Star.

66

Dreaming Of Stardom, A Distant Reverie Afar,

For Now, I Grace The Stage, In The Glow Of A Bar.

But It Won't Be Long, I Pen My Tune,

Crafting My Anthem, Something To Croon.

With Hopes It Resonates, A Chart-Topping Hit,

A Ticket To Fame, Where I Truly Fit.

Not Just A Face Lost In The Throng,

But A Luminary, Shining Bright And Strong.

Oh, How Sublime, If Fame Were Mine To Claim,

To Etch My Name In The Halls Of Fame.

Yearning For Connection, For Hearts To Know,

My Music, A Vessel, To Let Souls Freely Flow.

May My Sound Captivate, May It Astound,

And Spread Far And Wide, In Every Bound.

67

In My Chair, Reclined, Beneath The Night's Air,

I Tilt My Gaze Upward, To The Stars, I Stare.

Returned From The Bars, The Solitude I Own,

Embraced By Silence, I Am Alone.

No One To Disrupt, No Strife To Endure,

In This Solitary Realm, I Find My Allure.

No Ties To Bind, No Deceitful Cries,

In The Absence Of Company, My Spirit Flies.

For I Need No One But Myself To Embrace,

In My Solitude, I Find My Grace.

No Need For Conversation, For I Make Do,

With My Thoughts, My Musings, I Pursue.

No Conflicts To Engage, I Am Always In The Right,

In This Solitude, I Find My Might.

68

He's Walking Out From Those Prison Gates,
After Just Ten, His Freedom Awaits.

Though My Heart's Gutted, My Girly, My Pearl,
He's Out Too Early, My Anger Unfurl.

Swift Vengeance, My Soul Demands,
A Burden Lifted By His End In My Hands.

He Must Pay For His Grave Sin,
A Grin On My Face As I Watch Him Spin.

To See Him Fall Will Clear My Head,
With My Wrath, His Life I'll Shred.

No Other Path But To Take Him Down,
To Erase My Frown, To Wear His Crown.

I've Waited Too Long Since His Dark Crime,
To Even The Score, It's Now My Time.

With His Demise, He'll Hurt No More,

I'll Make My Stand, Settle The Score.

To Maintain My Sanity, I Must Inflict Pain,

With The Final Blow, I'll Silence His Disdain.

With Him On The Ground, My Mind's At Ease,

It's My Dream To Make Him Freeze.

I Want To See His Eyes As Life Bids Adieu,

For The Sake Of Her, So Dear, So True.

His Death Is Best To Protect The Rest,

For Her Sake, I'll Give My Best.

To End His Life, To Make Him Pay,

In A Lake, His Body Will Lay.

I'll Do The Deed, Let Nature Feed,

Nothing For Cops To Find, I'll Take The Lead.

I Hate To Break The Law, But I Saw His Claw,

I Hope God Forgives, And Not Strike With His Paw.

So I Sit In His House, Waiting For His Return,

My Resolve Firm, My Heart Ready To Burn.

As He Opens The Door, I Throw Him To The Floor,

With A Bat In My Hand, I Even The Score.

His Bones Break With Each Swing, Justice I Bring,

Blood Begins To Flow, My Vengeance Sings.

With Every Strike, I Feel So Right,

For Too Long, He's Caused Our Plight.

He Needs To Meet His End This Day,

I'll Have My Say, Come What May.

With Every Limb Broken, His Body Still,

I've Done What I Must, With An Iron Will.

His Last Breath Taken, His Life Forsaken,

I Relish His Demise, My Fury Unshaken.

As My Heart Slows, I Wipe The Blood Away,

My Hands Steady, For Justice Today.

69

In The Solemn Stillness Of The Night,

Life's Trials Cast A Shadow, Dark And Tight.

Yet Through The Storm, A Steadfast Smile I Bear,

A Beacon Of Hope In The Midst Of Despair.

Though Beaten And Bruised By Fate's Cruel Hand,

I Stand Resolute, A Soul To Understand.

No Collar Binds, No Master Claims My Will,

In Freedom's Embrace, I Rise And Fulfill.

The Light Reveals The Truth Within My Core,

A Tale Of Pride, Undimmed By Days Of Yore.

Though Shadows Creep And Linger In My Way,

My Spirit Shines, Unfaltering, As The Day.

Unbending, Unbroken, My Resolve Stands Tall,

Yet Whispers Of The End Softly Call.

In This Elegy, A Promise Lies Concealed,

A Heart Of Iron, By Time Revealed.

70

In The Sacred Vessel Of The Almighty Bowl,

Where My Pipe Becomes The Keeper Of My Soul.

I Bow To The Power Of Potent Pot,

Disregarding Constraints Of The Red Dot.

With It, I Transcend Any Potential Dud,

My Savior Lies Within The Green Bud.

I Stroll Upon Water, On Shards Of Glass,

With My Cherished Grass, I Surpass.

Witnessing Angels In A Dance,

In The Haze Of A Hash-Filled Trance.

71

Now I Grasp, His Presence Clear,

His Boundless Love, Ever Near.

In His Embrace, Forgiveness Thrives,

Through All My Days, As Long As I Strive.

No Need To Pursue, Or Chase His Grace,

It Flows Unbidden, In Every Place.

He Guides My Steps, Through Night And Day,

No Debts To Settle, No Price To Pay.

His Light Within, A Blazing Might,

In The Depths Of My Soul, He Takes Flight.

72

Silent Specters, Gliding By,

Invisible To The Naked Eye.

Elusive Beings, Best Left Alone,

Drifting In Realms Unknown.

They Hover In The Ether's Embrace,

Free From Earthly Concerns, In Grace.

No Pulse, No Breath, They Display,

Through Barriers, They Find Their Way.

Immune To True Death's Domain,

Bound To An Ethereal Plane.

73

Did You Catch Her Glide On By?

Damn, She Caught My Wandering Eye.

Each Step She Took Made My Heart Dance,

A Feat Of Grace, A Fleeting Chance.

Oh, How I Long For Her Embrace,

Yearning Fills This Empty Space.

Her Beauty, A Vision So Divine,

In My Dreams, I Wish She Were Mine.

With Every Glance, I Feel The Ache,

For Her, My Heart Would Gladly Break.

74

Pause And Ponder, Take A Breath,

Consider Deeply, Before You Quaff Death.

For Too Long You've Walked This Path,

It's Time To Veer From Its Wrath.

Set Aside The Bottle, Let It Be,

In Its Grip, You'll Never Be Free.

From Just One Taste, The Descent Begins,

Into A Spiral Of Darkness, Where Nobody Wins.

Refuse The Allure, The False Delight,

In Sobriety, Find Your True Might.

75

Onward I Journey, On This Quest,

Striving Always To Outdo The Rest.

Death Looms Close, Its Shadow Nigh,

A Constant Threat, The Reason Why.

My Level's At Stake, In Armor I Shake,

Each Step Forward, A Risk I Take.

I Feel The Wounds, Deep And Real,

In Dire Need Of A Healing Seal.

Beside Me, My Cleric, Unmoved It Seems,

As The Monster's Fury Upon Me Gleams.

One Bubble Of Life, A Precarious State,

For Both Me And My Foe, The Balance Of Fate.

Praying The Enemy Begins To Flee,

For Then, Victory Will Surely Be.

The Wizard's Magic, A Force To Be Cast,

To Vanquish This Beast, Its Reign At Last.

76

In The Earth, My Mushrooms Thrive,

A Psychedelic Spectacle They Contrive.

Brew The Tea, Sip And Behold,

Into Realms Unseen, Your Mind Unfold.

A Rush Of Euphoria, A Feeling So Grand,

As If You're Soaring, Weightless, Unplanned.

Sensations Emerge, With Each Subtle Wave,

In This Altered State, You're Truly Brave.

Shapes And Colors Dance Into View,

No Fear Holds Sway, As You Journey Anew.

77

Life's Journey, A Relentless Trial,

Yet Through It All, I'll Wear A Smile.

Though Battered And Bruised, I Stand Tall,

Not Chained Or Owned By Anyone's Thrall.

In The Glare Of Light, My Essence Revealed,

Yet My Pride Intact, My Fate Still Sealed.

I Refuse To Yield, To Bow Or Bend,

But Time's Grasp, It May Transcend.

78

See How I Sprint, Not For Jest,

But In Dire Flight, My Life's Behest.

Fleeing From Shadows, Strife's Cruel Knife,

Leaving Behind A Trail Of Life.

Pain I've Caused, A Heavy Stain,

For Scant Rewards, I Risk Disdain.

In Acts Of Theft, In Deeds Of Zeal,

Yet Hunger's Pang, It Cannot Heal.

Just Seeking To Endure, To Fly,

Amidst The Chaos, Reaching For The Sky.

79

Echoes Of Voices In My Mind's Abode,

Whispers Of Souls From Eras Old.

I Deem Them Ghosts Of Days Gone By,

Yet How Long Can This Reverie Fly?

Chatter Of Youth, Now A Distant Hum,

Once High Aloft, Now Lowly And Numb.

I Draw Near To The Earth's Cold Embrace,

Where Once I Soared, Now Confined In Space.

Lost In Shadows, Enveloped In Night,

The Future Appears Dim, Devoid Of Light.

Oh, To Turn Back Time, Rewrite The Past,

To Rearrange Life's Dice, And Make It Last.

But Innocence, Once Shed, Is Gone Forever,

A Return Denied, A Bond To Sever.

80

The Agony Within Me Churns,

A Signal That Something Yearns.

My Breath, A Shallow Stream Does Flow,

Heart's Rhythm, A Languid, Gentle Woe.

Vision Fades, Folds Into The Night,

A Chill Grips, Embracing Tight.

Struggling To Cling To Consciousness' Gate,

Tremors Ripple, A Tempest's Fate.

Like A Tire Spinning In A Rut,

I Sense A Tremor, A Jolt, A Gut.

Sound, Once Clear, Now Fades Away,

No Shred Of Doubt, Night Turns To Day.

Fear Floods In, An Overwhelming Tide,

As Thoughts Of Finality, No Longer Hide.

I've Rounded The Bend, Fate's Steady Trend,

And Soon, This Journey Finds Its End.

Part Five

81

I Hear The Train, Its Rumble Loud,

Even Over The Rain's Relentless Shroud.

Family's Arrival Looms, Not A Moment Too Soon,

No More Nights Spent Under The Pale Moon.

Though This Land May Seem Rough And Drear,

There's A Spirit Here That's Crystal Clear.

Boldly I Ventured, Seeking Fortune's Hold,

And With Grit And Sweat, My Gold I've Stowed.

Living Out West, Where Dreams Take Flight,

I've Risen To My Fullest Height.

Cheek Filled With Dip, A Habit Of The Land,

With A Gun On My Hip, I Make My Stand.

82

I Reach For My Gun, Swift And Sure,

As He Flees, His Fate Obscured.

He Won't Escape, He Must Atone,

For The Dangers He's Sown, He Must Be Shown.

Into The Store, His Refuge Sought,

But Danger Mounts, The Situation Fraught.

People Panic, Screams Fill The Air,

The Sound Of Alarm, A Piercing Blare.

Bodies Cower, Seeking Shelter Low,

Terrified By The Threat Of This Outlaw's Blow.

Behind The Racks, He Seeks His Flight,

But Out The Back, He'll Find No Respite.

I Must Confront Him, No Room To Doubt,

To Halt His Path, Justice To Sprout.

On His Heels, I Pursue With Zeal,

For The Weight Of Justice, He'll Surely Feel.

83

Observing The Storm As It Begins To Brew,

Life's Journey Unfolds, Anew.

Embarking On The Path To Truly Live,

To Share, To Give, To Generously Give.

Yet Sometimes, The Blows, They Come Unkind,

For Not Conforming, For Being Misaligned.

Silenced For Words, For Truths Too Loud,

Stabbed By Betrayal, Amidst The Crowd.

Blood Trickles, A Crimson Flow,

A The Waning Light, Does Show.

In The Final Moments, A Fleeting Chance,

To Glimpse The World In One Last Glance.

Heartbeats Drum, A Relentless Sound,

As The Wheel Of Time Spins Around.

A Shot Rings Out In The Shadow's Mark,

For Being Labeled As A Narc, In The Dark.

84

In The Land Of Lincoln Logs And Playful Pups,

Where Spinning Tops And Laughter Erupts.

But Choices Made Can Lead Astray,

To Paths Where Darkness Holds Sway.

Listen Closely To The Inner Voice,

For Heedless Acts Leave Little Choice.

Your Desires, Your Dreams, They Crash And Break,

Like Fragile China, No Longer Fake.

A Sentence Passed, A Life's Last Breath,

In The Cold Grip Of Impending Death.

85

Take A Moment, Just Be Still,

No Need To Rush, No Need To Thrill.

She's Not Your Match, Don't Lose Your Grip,

Don't Turn To Substances For A Fleeting Trip.

The Pipe's Allure, The Line's Deceit,

Temporary Solace, A Bitter-Sweet Retreat.

Drinking Deep Won't Heal Your Scars,

True Strength Lies Beyond The Bars.

Put Down The Knife, Don't Take That Road,

Resolve Conflict With Words, Not In Blood's Code.

For Once You Cross That Line So Red,

The Stains Of Guilt Will Haunt Your Head.

86

Their Eyes, Like Razors, Tear Me Up,

A Lost And Whimpering, Forsaken Pup.

Their Gaze, So Sharp, It Cuts My Soul,

In This Harsh World, I Seek Control.

I Feel Their Blades, They Pierce My Core,

In Shadows Deep, I Crave For More.

To Break These Chains, To Breathe, To See,

A Life Unbound, Where I Am Free.

My Spirit Bleeds, They Feast On Pain,

In Their Cruel Grip, I Fight In Vain.

They Strip Away My Heart, My Name,

Life's Bitter Truth, A Hollow Game.

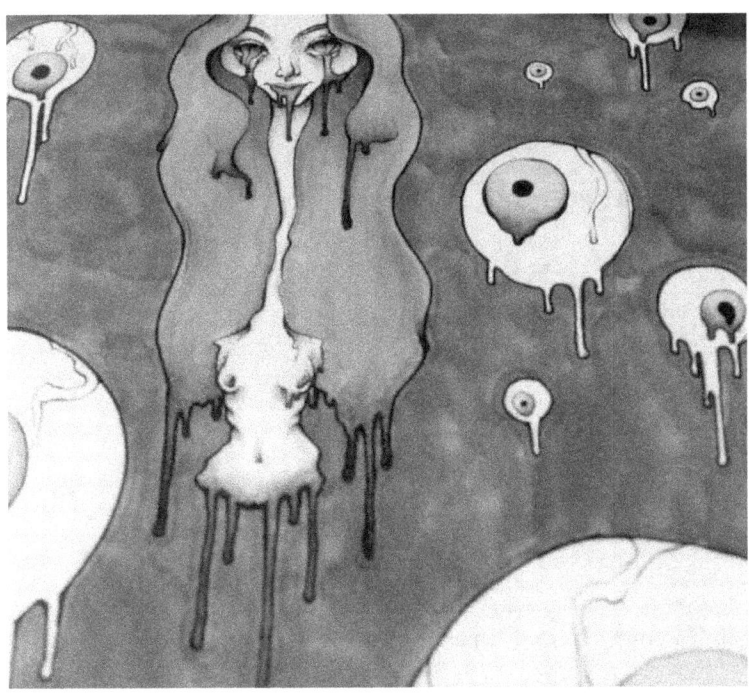

87

Life's Path, Not What You Once Sought,

True Happiness, It Can't Be Bought.

Destined For Greatness, Yet Feeling Sore,

In The Depths Of Despair, Life's Poor.

When The Darkness Clouds Your Sight,

The Urge To End It All Takes Flight.

Pain Becomes Your Constant Meal,

No Remedy Found To Truly Heal.

Yearning For That Final Reprieve,

In The Embrace Of Death, You Believe.

88

In The Somber Symphony Of The Rain's Refrain,

Echoes The Ache Of Too Much Pain.

It Rends The Soul, Tears Apart,

The Sorrow Swells, It's A Heavy Heart.

You Departed, Leaving Me Here,

In The Shadows, Consumed By Fear.

Navigating This World, Alone And Blue,

Without Your Presence, What Can I Do?

In This Vast Expanse, Love Seems Rare,

But Still, My Soul Seeks It Everywhere.

Like A Dove, My Spirit Soars,

Yearning For Love, It Implores.

Upward It Rises, Toward The Sky,

Seeking Solace, Longing To Fly.

89

In The Realm Of Fame, You Reign Supreme,

Where Every Soul Knows Your Esteemed Gleam.

Your Name, A Beacon In Every Home,

Echoes Of Your Deeds, Wherever They Roam.

Caught In The Shadows Of Drug-Fueled Nights,

You Shrug Off The Consequences With Casual Delights.

Scandalous Whispers Of Your Dalliance With Vice,

But You Wear It Like A Badge, Oh So Cool, So Precise.

Adolescents Idolize Your Every Move,

Blinded By Your Allure, They Fall Into Your Groove.

Yet Parents Lament, Your Image They Detest,

Protesting Your Influence, They Cannot Rest.

You're No Role Model, They Loudly Declare,

Guarding Their Children With Meticulous Care.

But Let The Youth Be, Set Them Free,

For In Your Grasp, Their Spirits May Flee.

Your Allure May Dazzle, But Beware,

For In Your Embrace, Their Wills You Ensnare.

90

Inject The Rush, Wear A Wicked Grin,
As The Poison Surges Within.

Heartbeat Races, Picking Up The Pace,
Lost In The Whirlwind Of This Chase.

Mind Adrift, Like A Ship At Sea,
In A Haze Of Euphoric Glee.

Breeze Through Your Hair, A Sensation Divine,
In This Moment, Ecstasy Intertwine.

Craving Intensifies, You Yearn For More,
Addiction's Grip Tightens, Its Hold You Abhor.

Trading Your Soul, In A Dangerous Game,
For A Fleeting High, You Carry The Shame.

Desperate Measures, You're Willing To Try,
Stealing, Cheating, Just To Satisfy.

Heroin Whispers, A Seductive Trend,

Binding You Closer, Until The Bitter End.

91

Commute To Toil, In Shadows He Waits,

Timing His Strike, Sealing My Fate.

Each Moment Ticking, Dropping The Dime,

My Life On A Thread, Running Out Of Time.

Around The Bend, My End Awaits,

An Accident Looms, Sealing My Dates.

Before The Noon Sun, My Destiny Sealed,

In The Clutches Of Fate, My Doom Revealed.

Struck By A Car, No Hospital Clear,

Behind The Wheel, My End Draws Near.

Death's Icy Grip, Now I Feel,

In The Realm Of Shadows, My Fate To Seal.

92

As The Drums Of War Beat Loud,

What's One More In The Crowd?

For Causes Undefined, We Wage,

A Bloody Tale On History's Page.

Our Sons And Daughters, Pawns Of Might,

In Politicians' Hands, They Fight.

In The Darkness Of The Night's Embrace,

Lies The Toll Of War, A Somber Grace.

Battles Rage, Governments Decree,

Truth Obscured, In Politics' Spree.

Press Machines, Fueled By Deceit,

Feed The Masses, A Bitter Treat.

Overhead, The Roar Of Planes,

Life's Fabric Torn, In Bombing Rains.

Bombs Descend With Deadly Haste,

Lives Shattered By The Blast's Cruel Taste.

Blameless Souls Caught In The Fray,

Victims Of Power's Deadly Play.

93

Board The Plane In Pouring Rain,

Bound For New York's Bustling Domain.

As It Ascends, Leaving Ground Behind,

Lightning Streaks, A Sight To Bind.

Thunder Roars, Storm's Fierce Cry,

In The Midst Of Chaos, We Fly.

Bolts Of Lightning, Jagged And Bold,

Strike The Plane, Its Metal Cold.

Fractured Skies, Chaos Unfurls,

As The Aircraft Begins To Twirl.

Heading Towards The Ocean's Vast Span,

A Journey's End, A Fate Unplanned.

94

I Lay My Bet, The Stakes Are Set,

With A Flicker, I Light My Cigarette.

I Study My Cards, Pondering Each,

Sipping My Drink, Calmness I Preach.

This Hand, I Pray, Must Come In Strong,

For In This Game, I've Been Strung Along.

Just One More Card, To Seal The Deal,

To Turn The Tide, And Make It Real.

My Hand Appears Promising, Fulfilling Dreams,

In This Moment, Nothing's As It Seems.

Confidence Surges, As I Stand,

Surely, Victory's Within My Hand.

I Place My Cards Down, Anticipation Profound,

Faces Around Me, Masks Of A Frown.

But Then It Happens, The Pot Is Mine,

In The Thrill Of Victory, I Shine.

95

Inhale That Hash, Feel The Rush,

A Fleeting High, A Whispered Hush.

Watch It All Flip, Reality's Grip,

As Flesh Begins To Tear And Rip.

The Vehicle Skids, On Its Side It Lies,

A Twisted Metal, Under Ominous Skies.

What A Ride, Through Chaos And Fear,

As Screams Mingle With The Crash's Sheer.

Blood Spills Forth, Life's Crimson Seed,

In This Moment, In Dire Need.

Help Is On Its Way, Sirens Blare,

Yet For Some, Life Hangs In Despair.

Not That You're Alive, But In This Fray,

Hope Still Lingers, In The Dimming Day.

96

In The Shadows Of His Past, He'd Roam,

Lost In Bottles, He Called His Home.

His Days Blurred By The Amber Gleam,

Caught In The Grip Of A Drunken Dream.

But One Dawn Broke, A Ray Of Light,

A Chance To Turn From Endless Night.

With Trembling Hands And Weary Soul,

He Sought A Path To Make Him Whole.

Through Valleys Deep And Mountains High,

He Faced His Demons, Refused To Lie.

With Every Step, He Left Behind

The Shackles Of His Troubled Mind.

With Courage As His Guiding Star,

He Journeyed Forth, Near And Far.

Through Storms Of Doubt A Raging Storm,

He Found His Strength, Returning To Form.

And In The Quiet Of His Newfound Grace,

He Learned To Stand In His Own Place.

No Longer Chained To Bottles Cold,

He Found His Worth, His Story Told.

With Each New Day, A Brighter Hue,

As He Embraced The World Anew.

With Every Heartbeat, A Fresh Start,

A Testament To His Brave Heart.

So Here's To Him, Who Dared To Fight,

And Found His Way Back To The Light.

A Man Reborn, His Spirit Free,

A Testament To Recovery.

97

Once Lost In Shadows, Now Bathed In Light,

Emerging From The Darkest Night.

A Phoenix Risen From Ashes Gray,

In The Dawn Of A Brand-New Day.

With Every Step, A Steady Stride,

No Longer Bound By Chains Inside.

Through Valleys Low And Mountains High,

He Soars Beneath The Endless Sky.

Each Breath A Gift, Each Heartbeat Strong,

In Harmony With Life's Sweet Song.

With Eyes Wide Open, He Sees Anew,

The Beauty In Each Morning Dew.

No Longer Ruled By Craving's Call,

He Stands Tall, Unbroken, Standing Tall.

With Newfound Purpose, He Walks The Earth,

A Testament To His Rebirth.

For Every Battle, Every Scar,

Has Shaped Him Into Who You Are.

With Courage As His Guiding Light,

He Faces Each Day Without Fright.

So Here's To Life After The War,

To Finding Peace And So Much More.

A Journey Long, Yet Worth The Fight,

In The Brilliance Of Newfound Light.

98

In The Shadows Deep, Where Demons Dwell,

Lies A Tale Of Darkness, A Haunting Spell.

Where Souls Are Lost In A Twisted Dance,

Ensnared By The Grip Of Drug's Cruel Trance.

It Starts With A Whisper, A Seductive Call,

A Fleeting Escape From Life's Bitter Thrall.

But Soon It Consumes, Like A Raging Fire,

Leaving Behind Only Ashes And Mire.

At First, It Whispers, Promises Sweet,

But Soon It Devours, Soul, Does Cheat.

It Steals Your Joy, Your Hopes, Your Dreams,

Leaving Behind Shattered, Silent Screams.

The Needle's Sting, The Pill's Deceit,

Each High A Lie, Each Low Complete.

Families Torn, Relationships Strained,

In The Wake Of Addiction's Pain.

From Euphoria's Peak To Despair's Abyss,

It's A Journey Paved With False Bliss.

Where Every Fix Is A Desperate Plea,

For A Fleeting Moment Of Numb Reprieve.

Yet Beneath The Haze, A Flicker Remains,

A Spark Of Hope Amidst The Chains.

For In The Darkest Depths, Light Can Survive,

In The Silence, Whispers Of Hope Are Alive.

So Reach Out A Hand To Those Who Fall,

For In Compassion, Lies The Cure For All.

Let's Break The Cycle, Break The Chain,

And Heal The Wounds Of Addiction's Bane.

99

In Shadows Deep, Where Sorrow Dwells,
A Man In Despair, His Story Tells.
With Heavy Heart And Burdened Soul,
He Wanders Lost, Without Control.

Through Valleys Dark, He Roams Alone,
His Heart Aches With A Heavy Groan.
In The Silence Of The Night's Embrace,
He Seeks Solace In An Empty Space.

His Laughter Lost, His Smile Worn Thin,
His Spirit Crushed By Pain Within.
Each Step He Takes, A Heavy Tread,
As He Carries The Weight Of Words Unsaid.

The World Around Him Fades To Gray,
As Hope Seems But A Distant Ray.
He Longs For Peace, For Release From Strife,
To Find Reprieve From This Weary Life.

Yet In The Depths Of Despair's Embrace,

A Glimmer Of Light, A Saving Grace.

For Even In Darkness, Hope Can Bloom,

And Lead Him From His Endless Gloom.

So Let Us Reach Out, Lend A Hand,

And Help Him Rise, Help Him Stand.

For In Our Love, He'll Find Repair,

And Break Free From The Grip Of Despair.

100

In Shadows Deep, Where Demons Hide,

A Soul Ensnared By The Heroin's Tide.

In Veins, The Poison Finds Its Way,

A Fleeting Escape, A Price To Pay.

With Every Hit, A Fleeting High,

Yet Deeper Still, The Cravings Lie.

In Shadows Lurk The Darkest Fears,

And Agony Drips With Silent Tears.

The Needle's Sting, The Rush's Embrace,

A Moment's Solace, A Fleeting Grace.

But In Its Wake, A Hollow Shell,

A Prisoner Trapped In A Living Hell.

Lost In A Haze Of Numbing Bliss,

Reality Fades With Every Kiss.

But Beneath The Surface, A Soul Cries Out,

Longing For Freedom From The Endless Bout.

For Every Fix, A Piece Is Lost,

A Soul Adrift, A Heavy Cost.

Yet Even In The Depths Of Despair,

There Lies A Glimmer, A Hope To Repair.

So Let Us Reach Out, Lend A Hand,

And Help Reclaim What's Been Unmanned.

For In Compassion's Light, There's A Chance To Save,

A Heroin Addict From An Early Grave.

Part Six

101

In The Quiet Before The Storm Begins,

There's A Whisper That Sometimes Wins.

Addiction, They Say, Is A Beast In The Night,

But Listen Closely—It's Also A Fight.

A Fight For The Morning We Wish To See,

A Battle With Shadows We Long To Be Free.

It Starts With A Sip, A Smoke, A Small Bet,

A Gamble With Destiny, A Dance With Regret.

It's The Allure Of The Escape, The Promise Of Bliss,

An Oasis In Deserts, A Serpent's Hiss.

We're Drawn To The Fire, Though We Know We'll Burn,

For In The Flicker Of Flames, We See A Chance To Turn.

Turn Away From The Pain, The Sorrow, The Loss,

But The Bridge We Cross Is Covered In Moss.

Slippery, Uncertain, With Each Step We Take,

We're Gambling With Pieces Of Our Soul At Stake.

Addiction Isn't Choosy, It Loves Us All The Same,

Rich Or Poor, Young Or Old, It's A Democratic Game.

It Whispers Sweet Nothings, Promises Of Power,

But Leaves Us In Ruins, A Wilted, Dying Flower.

Yet, Here's The Thing About The Night, It Always Ends,

And With The Dawn, A Message The Universe Sends.

Hope Is A Phoenix, From Ashes, It Rises,

Offering Us A Chance At New Disguises.

Recovery, A Journey, A Path Less Trod,

It's Rocky, It's Steep, But It's A Path To God.

A God Of Our Understanding, A Higher Power,

A Force That Blooms Within, A Resilient Flower.

So Let's Talk About Addiction, Not As A Chain,

But As A Chapter In Our Story, A Momentary Rain.

For After The Storm, The Air Is Clear,

And What Was Once Distant, Is Suddenly Near.

This Is Not A Solo Journey, We Walk Hand In Hand,

With Those Who've Traversed This No Man's Land.

Together, We're Stronger, A Formidable Crew,

With Love, Understanding, And Perspectives Anew.

So Here's To The Fighters, The Warriors, The Brave,

Dancing With Shadows, The Lives They Save.

Addiction, You May Have Started The War,

But We're The Authors Of This Lore.

We Write Our Endings, We Define Our Fate,

With Courage, With Kindness, We Navigate.

This Spoken Word, A Testament, A Declaration,

To The Spirit Of Survival, A Standing Ovation.

To All Those Fighting Battles Unseen,

Remember, You're A King, You're A Queen.

In The Tapestry Of Life, Every Thread Is Needed,

With Love, With Grace, We Have Succeeded.

102

In Sorrow's Deep Embrace, I Lie,

A Shadowed Heart, I Wonder Why.

For Deeds Ill Done, I Mourn The Past,

Yet Hope The Pain Will Never Last.

This Moment's Gloom Shall Fade Away,

As Morning Brings A Brighter Day.

In Fields Of Green, My Soul Shall Play,

Where Laughter Drives The Tears Away.

With Every Effort, Striving High,

Yet Faltering Beneath The Sky.

Though Errors Haunt, I Strive Anew,

To Live Each Day With Heart And True.

In Nature's Arms, I Find My Peace,

A Gentle Balm, My Soul's Release.

The Grass Beneath, The Sky Above,

Reminds Me Of A Boundless Love.

103

In My Chair, I Feel The Glare,

Her Pain Revealed, Nothing To Spare.

Tears Flow, A Torrent Of Fears,

Injustice Grips, Injustice Sears.

Hooded Now, Unjustly Accused,

Fear Consumes, Truth Refused.

Straps Tighten, Terror's Hold,

Dimming Lights, Futures Untold.

104

Sales Soaring High, Beyond They Should,

Hard Work, The Key, All Understood.

In Wealth, We Thrive, Honey's Delight,

Life's Grandeur, Hand In Hand, Takes Flight.

Our Efforts Yield, As We Pursue,

Success In Reach, Dreams Coming True.

With Riches Earned, Our Love's Embrace,

In Abundance, Life's Joys We Chase.

105

Hear My Voice, In Whispers Deep,

Feel My Curves, In Shadows Steep.

Turn The Light, To Night's Embrace,

Let Desire, Find Its Place.

Make It Rough, With Fervent Might,

For I Am Strong, In Passion's Light.

Flames Of Yearning, Set Ablaze,

Like A Pyre, In Moonlit Haze.

Burn With Fervor, Fierce And Wild,

In This Dance, Where Love Beguiled.

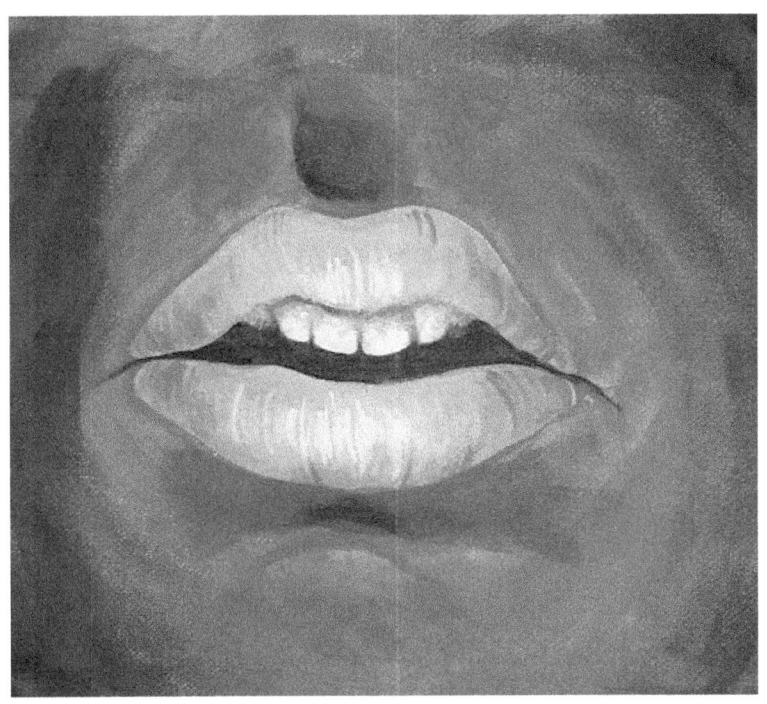

106

Feeling Aligned, With All Your Might,

From Pills You Bite, May Spark A Fight.

Be It Black Or White In Your Sight,

From Any Height, No Fear Takes Flight.

Yet In The Darkness, No Light In Sight,

Spite Clouds Your Mind, In Endless Night.

Fists Clenched Tight, In Anger's Might,

Eyes Open Slightly, Not Polite.

In This Storm, You're Set To Smite,

Flying High, Like A Kite In Flight.

107

Emerging From The Daze, A Fog Still Lies,

Last Night's Tumult, A Storm In Disguise.

Rough Was The Journey, No Glimpse Of Light,

In The Midst Of Chaos, Struggling In The Night.

I Was Loud, I Confess, No Pride To Wield,

Moments Lost In Tumult, Emotions Unsealed.

Carried Away On Currents, Swift And Strong,

Control Slipping, With No Pause, No Song.

In The Blink Of An Eye, The Rush Overcasts,

Yet In That Whirlwind, Oh What A Blast!

108

You Don't See Me, So Let Me Be,

In Shadows Cast, Where None Can See.

I'm Tired Of Being Just A Toy,

For A Heartless, Foolish Boy.

Your Desires Shallow, Cold As Stone,

Seeking Flesh, But Not The Bone.

All You Crave Is Lust's Cruel Fuck,

But Now, My Dear, You're Out Of Luck.

In Silence, I Reclaim My Name,

No Longer Bound By Your Cruel Game.

My Spirit Rises, Fierce And Free,

Unseen By You, But Known To Me.

In This Elegy, My Heart Will Soar,

A Soul Unchained, Forevermore.

109

In My Chair, I Sit And Stare,

Life's Unfairness, Heavy In The Air.

With Each Sip I Take, I Sink,

In This Cycle, I Find No Link.

Bottles Scattered, A Chaotic Sight,

Their Contents Spilled, Staining The Night.

Oh, How I Long For Her To Be Near,

But In Her Absence, I Find Solace In Beer.

110

Their Eyes, Like Razors, Tear Me Up,

A Lost And Whimpering, Forsaken Pup.

Their Gaze, So Sharp, It Cuts My Soul,

In This Harsh World, I Seek Control.

I Feel Their Blades, They Pierce My Core,

In Shadows Deep, I Crave For More.

To Break These Chains, To Breathe, To See,

A Life Unbound, Where I Am Free.

My Spirit Bleeds, They Feast On Pain,

In Their Cruel Grip, I Fight In Vain.

They Strip Away My Heart, My Name,

Life's Bitter Truth, A Hollow Game.

111

Oz Fest Eluded Our Eager Quest,

Yet We Persisted, Giving Our Best.

Blocked By Gates, Our Passage Denied,

Disdain For Authority, We Couldn't Hide.

Bill's Stash, Uncovered, A Bitter Pill,

Our Sins Unveiled, Our Hopes Stood Still.

Denied Entry, For Our Transgressions' Sake,

Our Oz Fest Dreams Shattered In Our Wake.

112

Seizing The Gun, A Game Begun,

With One Bullet, Our Courage Spun.

Spinning The Wheel, Emotions High,

What Fate Awaits, We Can't Deny.

Pulling The Trigger, Nerves A-Stir,

In This Gamble, Who Will Confer?

Challenging Fate, With Every Breath,

In This Moment, Dance With Death.

113

In A Land Where Shadows Draped The Sunlit Skies,

Lived Souls Ensnared By Whispering Lies.

In The Heart Of This Desolate, Forsaken Place,

Was A Struggle Of Wills, A War To Face.

Once A Beacon Of Hope, Now Dimmed By Despair,

He Stood On The Edge, Gasping For Air.

His Heart Raced As His Fear Gripped His Mind,

Now Lost In The Mire, By The War Defined.

He Wandered Through Life With Dreams, Praise,

But The Dragon Of Darkness Set His Soul Ablaze.

A Substance, A Savior, A False Reprieve,

From The Pain And The Sorrow, He Couldn't Leave.

In The Alleys And Corners, Where Light Feared To Tread,

He Found Companions, Equally Led.

They Shared Tales Of Woe, Of Dreams Once Bright,

Now Shattered And Broken, Lost To The Night.

Through Needles And Powders, In Smoke And In Drink,

They Sought Solace In Darkness, On The Brink.

But The Dragon Was Hungry, Its Appetite Vast,

Consuming Their Spirits, It Held Them Fast.

Ethan's Eyes Once Sparkled With Youthful Gleam,

Now Dulled By The Nightmare, Devoid Of Dream.

His Family's Voices, Distant And Faint,

Called Out In Anguish, In Sorrow And Plaint.

In The Grip Of His Torment, He Wandered Alone,

Through Valleys Of Agony, Flesh And Bone.

He Saw Visions Of Past, Of Love And Of Light,

But The Dragon's Whisper Promised Respite.

Days Turned To Nights, In An Endless Blur,

His Mind, A Tempest, His Heart, A Stir.

But Deep In The Silence, A Spark Remained,

A Whisper Of Hope, Though Faint And Strained.

A Woman Of Grace, With A Heart Pure And Kind,

Reached Out To Ethan, In His Troubled Mind.

Her Name Was Grace, And Her Eyes Held A Fire,

A Promise Of Life, Beyond The Mire.

She Spoke Of Redemption, Of Battles Won,

Of Rising Anew, Like The Morning Sun.

She Held His Hand Through The Darkest Of Nights,

Guiding Him Gently To The Dawning Light.

With Each Step He Took, The Dragon Did Roar,

But Ethan, Determined, Fought Evermore.

Through Tears And Through Pain, He Found His Way,

To A Life Reborn, To A Brighter Day.

No Longer A Prisoner To The Dragon's Might,

He Stood Tall And Proud, In The Morning Light.

His Journey Of Sorrow, Of Struggle And Strife,

Now A Testament To The Power Of Life.

In The Annals Of Time, His Story Remains,

Of A Soul Once Lost, Freed From Its Chains.

An Epic Of Darkness, Of Battles Fought,

And The Victory Of Light, Where Hope Is Sought.

114

In The Dim-Lit Room Where Stories Unfold,

Where Weary Souls Gather, Both Young And Old,

Hope Whispers Softly, A Gentle Reprieve,

In The Circle Of Courage, We Learn To Believe.

Through Tales Of Struggle, Of Nights Dark And Cold,

We Share Our Burdens, Our Secrets Untold,

Yet In Each Confession, A Spark Starts To Glow,

A Beacon Of Light, A Path We Now Know.

With Hands Clasped In Unity, Strength We Do Find,

In The Fellowship's Warmth, We Leave Pain Behind,

For In Every Meeting, A Promise Is Made,

Of Brighter Tomorrows, Where Shadows Will Fade.

One Step At A Time, We Reclaim Our Days,

With Each Sober Breath, We Mend Broken Ways,

Together We Rise, From Ashes We Grow,

In The Embrace Of AA, New Life We Bestow.

So Here's To The Journey, The Trials We Face,

To The Laughter And Tears, And Each Small Grace,

For In This Brave Circle, We Find Our Way,

In The Heart Of AA, Hope Comes To Stay.

115

In Shadows Deep, Where Darkness Reigns,

A Soul Once Lost, Bound By Chains,

In Labyrinths Of Despair And Night,

It Wandered Far From Hope's Bright Light.

Amid The Murk And Sorrow's Mire,

A Flicker Sparked, A Faint Desire,

A Whisper Soft, A Call To Be,

The Dawn That Waits Beyond The Sea.

In Nights Of Pain And Days Of Gloom,

Where Silence Echoed Like A Tomb,

A Glimmer Grew, A Star To Guide,

Through Tempest Wild, And Rising Tide.

Upon The Shore Of Broken Dreams,

Where Nothing Is Quite As It Seems,

A Voice Emerged, Both Strong And Clear,

Rise Up, Dear Heart, And Conquer Fear.

With Trembling Step, The Path Begun,

A Journey Toward The Rising Sun,

Through Valleys Low And Mountains High,

With Hope Reborn And Spirits Nigh.

The Shadows Clawed, They Fought To Stay,

Yet Light Endured And Paved The Way,

For Every Tear And Every Fall,

Gave Strength To Rise Above It All.

In Fellowship Of Kindred Souls,

Who Shared The Burden, Shared The Goals,

Together Bound By Common Fight,

They Walked As One Into The Light.

The Road Was Long, The Trials Fierce,

Yet Through The Dark, Their Hearts Did Pierce,

With Every Step, With Every Breath,

They Moved Away From Grips Of Death.

And There Amid The Twilight's Glow,

A Garden Bloomed, A Peaceful Show,

Of Flowers Bright And Waters Clear,

Of Melodies To Soothe The Ear.

Serenity, Like Morning Dew,

In Gentle Whispers, Softly Grew,

It Wrapped Around, A Tender Grace,

And Healed The Wounds Time Could Not Erase.

In Meadows Wide, They Found Their Peace,

A Life Reborn, A Sweet Release,

From Chains That Held And Shadows Deep,

They Woke To Dreams They Dared To Keep.

Now Standing Tall, With Eyes That Gleam,

No Longer Trapped In Endless Dream,

With Hope As Bright As Morning Sun,

They See The Battles They Have Won.

For In The Heart Of Every Storm,

A Quiet Strength Begins To Form,

And Through The Trials, Hope Will Rise,

Like Dawn Upon The Darkest Skies.

So Hear This Tale Of Night To Day,

Of Hope And Love That Lights The Way,

For In Each Heart, A Dawn Will Break,

And With Its Light, New Paths We'll Take.

116

In Shadows Where The Lost Souls Dwell,

Lies A Chain That Pulls Them Down To Hell.

With Every Link, A Promise Broken,

A Silent Plea, A Word Unspoken.

This Chain, It's Made Of Dreams And Dust,

Of Shattered Trust And Chemical Lust.

It Tightens With Each Desperate Fix,

In A Cycle That's Impossible To Nix.

117

There's A Thief That Roams The Streets At Night,

Stealing More Than Just The Morning's Light.

It Takes Your Joy, Your Peace, Your Will,

Leaves You Empty, Cold, And Still.

This Thief, It's Known By Many Names,

But The Pain It Brings Always Remains.

It's Addiction, Cruel And Bleak,

Leaving Even The Strongest Feeling Weak.

118

Within The Silence, Screams Are Loud,

As Chains Of Addiction Hold Them Bound.

They Fight, They Struggle, They Gasp For Air,

Trapped In A Nightmare, Lost In Despair.

Their Voices Echo In A Void,

Their Lives, By Drugs, Are Now Destroyed.

Yet Hope Whispers, Soft And Slight,

Guiding Them Through The Darkest Night.

119

The Fiercest Battles Are Not Seen,

They're Fought In Minds, In Spaces Between.

Where Addiction Wrestles With The Soul,

And Taking Back Control Is The Ultimate Goal.

Each Day Is A Step, A Chance To Fight,

To Move From Darkness Into Light.

Though The Path Is Long And Filled With Pain,

It's There That Lost Dreams Will Reign.

120

In The Mirror, A Stranger Stares,

A Shadow Of Themselves, Caught Unawares.

Drugs Have Stolen So Much Away,

Leaving A Husk, In Dismay.

Yet In Those Eyes, A Spark Remains,

A Reminder Of The Love That Sustains.

The Journey Back Is Hard And Long,

But Love's Reflection Makes Them Strong.

121

Addiction Is A Storm That Rages,

Tearing Through The Book Of Life's Pages.

It Leaves Behind A Trail Of Tears,

A Testament To Wasted Years.

But After Every Storm, The Sky Clears,

Offering A Chance To Face One's Fears.

In The Aftermath, There's A Chance To Rebuild,

To Fulfill The Dreams That Drugs Had Stilled.

122

Ghosts Walk Among Us, Unseen, Unheard,

Their Lives By Addiction Are Blurred.

Chasing A High, They've Lost Their Way,

Becoming Shadows, Day By Day.

Yet, These Ghosts Are Not Beyond Reach,

With Love And Care, We Can Breach.

The Walls They've Built, Brick By Brick,

And Help Them Heal, Slow And Quick.

123

A Cycle Vicious, Hard To Break,

Leaves Behind An Endless Wake.

Addiction's Grip, Tight And Cruel,

Makes Breaking Free A Grueling Duel.

But Cycles Can Be Stopped In Tracks,

With Determination, One Can Hack.

The Chains That Bind, The Ties That Hold,

And Step Into A Future Bold.

124

At A Crossroads, Every Addict Stands,

Choices Pulled In Many Strands.

One Path Leads To Further Decay,

The Other, A Chance To Break Away.

It's Here, In This Moment Of Choice,

That One Must Listen To The Inner Voice.

Forsake The Path Of Addictions Might

And To Choose The Path That Leads To Light.

125

From The Ashes Of Addiction, A New Life Can Rise,

A Journey Of Struggle, Of Lows And Highs.

With Every Step, A Victory Small,

Proof That One Can Overcome It All.

Rebirth Is Not Merely A Chance To Live,

But An Opportunity To Forgive,

To Build Anew, To Love, To Dream,

And To Flow Once More With Life's Stream.

Haiku of an Addict

Part I

1

Snort A Line of Coke

Feeling Numbness In My Nose

I Feel The Rush Hit

2

Body Is Shaking

I'm Tilting The Bottle Back

Calm Begins To Take

3

Feeling That Rush Now

Flying Higher Than Before

Crashing Back To Soon

4

I Embrace My Sin

Heart And Soul Are Void Of Light

God, Forsaken Me

5

My Death Approaches

The Straps Firmly Tightened Down

Injections Begin

6

Shot Down Like A Dog

Have Been Hunted For So Long

Unable To Flee

7

Locked Within A Cell

Forced To Live In A Prison

Body, Heart, Mind, and Soul

8

His Almighty Grace

Light Illuminating All

Clearing Out Darkness

9

I Must Be Insane

Cannot Stop All The Voices

Always There Waiting

10

The Gun In My Mouth

The Tears Drip Off Of My Face

I Pull The Trigger

11

Waiting For The Start

Tonight, The Engines Rev High

Clutch Drops, The Car Goes

12

Freedom, A Mindset

Prison, A Reality

Death, A Welcome Fate

13

Try To Tap The Vein

Have To Chase That High Again

I Want It... Need It

14

Stabbed Hard In The Chest

Ripping Through Tormented Soul

Relieving Life's Pain

15

Picking At My Skin

Haven't Slept So Many Days

My Body Rotting

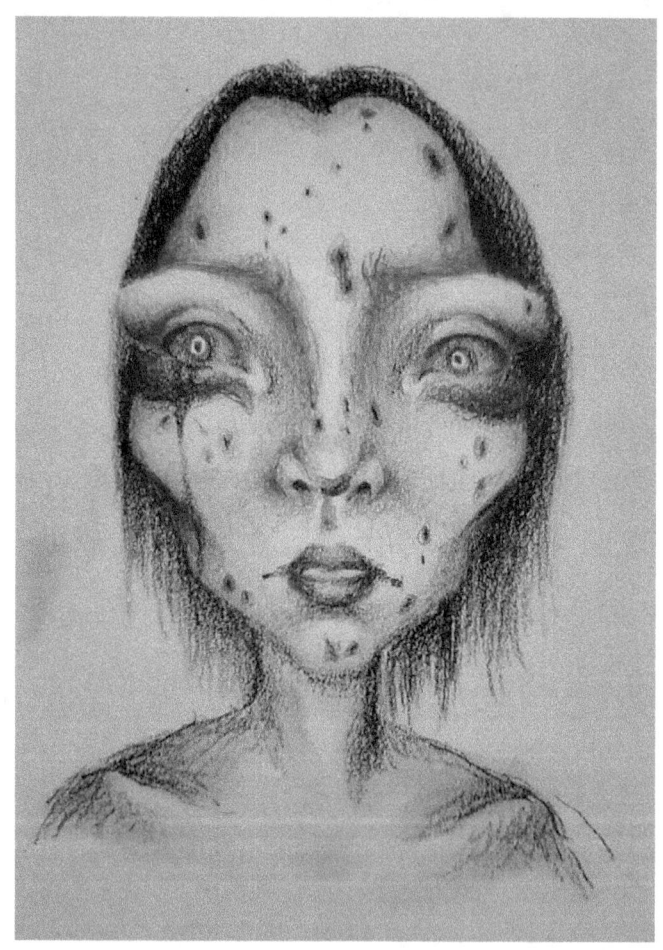

16

Feeling Fucking Free

Just Falling, Soaring, Flying

Ground Rushing Up Fast

17

Wondering Around

Their Souls Trapped In A Shell

The Living Dead Walk

18

Drinking My Cold Beer

Washing Away My Deep Fear

My Eyes Do So Tear

19

Snort The White Powder

My Nose Always Goes So Numb

I Now Own The World

20

I Feel So Sickened

Cold Sweat Drips Down My Forehead

Where Is My Dealer

21

Trapped In My Dark Cell

Imprisoned In My Own Mind

The Screams Never Stop

22

Laying In The Street

Blood Spilling From My Split Head

Left To Die Again

23

I Feel Satan's Grip

Entered My Soul On A Trip

Will Never Let Go

24

Wondering Around

Homeless Living On The Street

The Wondering Dead

25

Falling Through The Cracks

Struggling Just To Live My Life

Lost In The System

26

Misery Of Life

Piercing My Soul To The Core

Beaten Down By Life

27

Clean And Free At Last

Sobriety Is My Air

I Can Breathe Again

28

A Sweet Kid He Was

He Snapped Like An Animal

Put Down Like A Dog

29

Parents Dead So Long

Became A Loner In Life

Hiding From The World

30

Caught In Your Own Lies

Living The Lies In Your Head

Wondering And Lost

31

Falling From The Sky

Wind Rustling By Very Fast

Soaring Like A Bird

32

Gods Loving Light Shines

Shown Down On So Many Souls

But It's Lost On Me

33

Needle Stuck In Arm

Drugs Flowing Freely Through Me

My Life Is My Death

34

Stuck Out In The Woods

My Mind Is Like A Forrest

Trees Fall Silently

35

Like Being Alone

Far From All Other People

Just Living For Me

36

Helping People Live

Saving Their Eternal Soul

Gods Servants To Man

37

Deep Within My Head

I Know I Fuel Hatred

Poison In My Veins

38

Hide Under The Bed

Saw The Splattering of Red

They Are Surely Dead

39

I Hear The Siren

Blackness Entering Vision

Will They Be In Time

40

My Father Of Mine

So Much More To Give Us All

Died Too Soon In Life

Part II

41

Seeing A Future

Remembering All The Past

Celebrating Life

42

Trapped In A Dark Mine

Engulfed In Total Darkness

Struggling To Just Breathe

43

I Hear The Motors

Running Of The World Machine

Stop Them If I Could

44

Send Boys To Slaughter

Creating War Among Men

The Leaders Of Man

45

Now Missing My Legs

Lost In A Fight For Freedom

Doing The Right Thing

46

Returning From War

Adjusting To My New Life

Patient Is My Wife

47

Lost In Deep Dark Thought

Now Searching For Something More

Not Sure What To Do

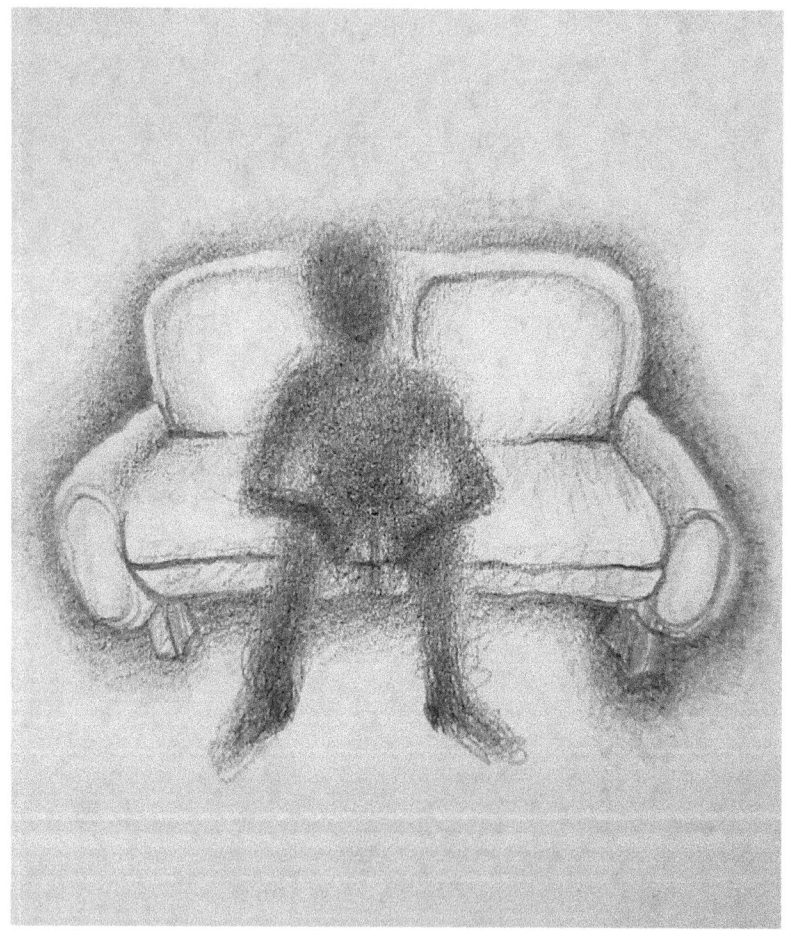

48

Drugs On The Corner

Someone Is Going To Gain

Money Over Life

49

True In My Own Mind

Singing A Different Tune

It Will Change This Time

50

Domestic Terror

Drugs Flowing Like A River

Shattering Our Youth

51

Skipping Rocks All Day

Lost In My Young Childhood Youth

Not Knowing The World

52

Playing With Others

Difficult To Get Along

Children Filled With Hate

53

Dying Like Embers

Taken Over By The Drugs

Dealers Peddle Them

54

Seeing Clouds Above

The Soaring Of A White Dove

Gods Eternal Love

55

I Am Who I Am

I'm Not A Religious Man

I Give My Own Peace

56

Not Looking To Die

But It Will Come For Us All

I Do Not Feel Fear

57

Tears Run From Her Eye

Looking At Her Dead Husband

Sorrow In Her Heart

58

Like Little Lost Sheep

They Are Slaughtered In Their Sleep

Pain Running So Deep

59

Traded My Own Soul

For Riches, Bitches, And Fame

A Hollywood Life

60

Crazy As A Fox

My Own Lies Always Be True

President Am I

61

Dumbass Liberals

Not Seeing The Real World

Living Delusion

62

Right Against The Left

Neither Will Bend Anymore

The Real Problem

63

Never Seen Again

Live On In Our Memory

Are The Good Old Days

64

Our Sad Broken World

Violence On All Levels

Nothing New To Us

65

Smoker, A Toker

Burning Well Past My Midnight

I'm Living My Life

66

I'm Out In The Black

Free To My Own Way Of Life

To Me Flying Free

67

You Always Tell Me

How Am I Suppose To Feel

But I'm Not Able

68

The Big Tree Falls Down

Hear It Crash To The Hard Ground

But I Am Alone

69

If The Water Leaks

And The Candle Light Is Fire

Maybe All Is Lost

70

Randomness of Death

Can Strike Out All Of Mankind

Where Is Your Soul Now

71

Thoughtless People Live

Living Amongst All Of Us

Using Up Our Air

72

Danger In Our Air

Toxic And Deadly Terror

The Weapons Of Death

73

A Shortness of Breath

Shooting Pain Starts Down Your Arm

The Reaper Watches

74

My Body Is Trapped

My Mind Is My Own Temple

I Am Free To Think

75

At Its Beck And Call

Still Chained Like An Animal

I Can't Put It Down

76

I Feel The Power

It's Cold But Embraces Me

My One Friend, My Gun

77

Beer Is So Tasty

I Like Beer And It Likes Me

Beer Is My Best Friend

78

I Lay Here In Bed

Facing The Reaper Of Death

He Now Laughs At Me

79

Caught In The Middle

A Child Used As A Weapon

No One Cares For Them

Part III

80

The Picture Doesn't Show

The Dread In My Eyes And Soul

Beaten Night And Day

81

Two Men Still Fighting

Both Refusing To Give In

Will We Always Watch

82

I Hear The Angels

In The Laughter Of Children

It Always Fades Out

83

Passion Of The Youth

Builds Worlds And Can Move Mountains

The Old Bring Despair

84

Life Evolves With Us

A Bitterness Breeds With Age

Death Becomes Freedom

85

With Age Comes Wisdom

With Wisdom Comes One's Purpose

With Purpose Comes Life

86

Not About Nature

But It Is Still A Haiku

Fucking Deal With It

87

A Ship Lost At Sea

Waves Crashing Over The Bow

Death Awaits For Them

88

Plane Is Going Down

People Praying In Their Seats

Too Little Too Late

89

I Open My Chute

Falling Down Into The DMZ

Entering Combat

90

Waiting By The Phone

Wondering If She'll Call Back

Silence Is Endless

91

Watching For The Light

Lost In My Hidden Dark Place

Smothering Darkness

92

Filled With Rage And Hate

Joy Of Pain And Suffering

Causing Wounds To Man

93

Eyes Bleary And Red

The Crown is Heavy And Worn

Victory Is Near

94

Bound By A Blood Oath

Sworn To Die And To Protect

Saving The Princess

95

Plague Begins To Spread

Across The Air And The Sea

Ending The Known World

96

Waves Crash On The Shore

Wind Gusts Across The Ocean

Clouds Turn Dark And Gray

97

Strapped On A Table

Sentence Being Carried Out

My Death Is Coming

98

The Clock Stares At Me

It's Ticking Down Till The End

Life Ebbing Away

99

Lost In The Desert

Searching For Water, For Food

Sun Draining My Life

100

Running Wild Tonight

I'm Higher Than I Should Be

Loving This Moment

101

Traded In My Soul

Living The Corporate World

Money Is My God

102

Life Feeling Empty

Since She Was Taken Away

Trying To Find Peace

103

War Of All Nations

Over Religious Dogma

Peace Is Without God

104

Nations Torn Apart

Disease Ravaging The Poor

Third World Suffering

105

Decided To Go

Grateful For What We Once Had

Must Choose To Go On

106

Hitting The Pipe Hard

Feeling The Train In My Head

Craving My Cocaine

107

Seeing The Blue Skies

Feeling Free As I Take Flight

Soaring Through The Air

108

Living In The Camp

Captured By A Crazy Man

Double Eight Of Hate

109

Grape Of The Mad Dog

Prefer Milk Of The Poppy

But Anything Works

110

Wondering Around

Finding Something To Live For

My Soul Finding Peace

111

My Head Is Pounding

Feels Like I Have Been Beaten

Body Shutting Down

112

Laying In Gutter

Piece Of Trash In The Bayou

Just Like The City

113

Leaves Fluttering Down

The Wind Blows Freely In Gusts

The Sun Shines Brightly

114

The Stars Out Of Reach

Long To Return To The Sky

Stranded, Stuck, Lost, Dead

115

The Funeral Pyre

Burns High In The Dark Night Sky

Valhalla He Goes

116

Set Off From The Shore

Look To Pillage And Plunder

Ah, The Pirate's Life

117

Sweat Lining My Brow

Dilated And Blurry Eyes

Just Living The Life

118

Heart Beating, Racing

Adrenaline Speeding Through

The Rush Of Power

119

Poor Mother Nature

Feeling The Pain Of The World

Living The Slow Death

120

Laying In A Bath

Red Starts Filling The Water

Life Ebbing Away

121

Looking At People

I Think It's Kind Of Funny

How Dumb They Can Be

122

Is Full Of Self Doubt

Every Time He Sees Himself

Unsure Of His Life

123

Lost In Emotion

Has Forgotten Who He Was

Grief Stricken His Heart

124

Living My Life Clean

I Found My Serenity

Seeing Things Clearly

125

Killer Of Giants

Metal Mountains Of Madness

Still Flexing Their Might

126

The End Is Coming

For My Heart, Mind, And My Soul

I Embrace What Comes

127

Flying Like A Dove

Soaring Through The Open Sky

Peace, Serenity

128

Innocence Is Lost

Buried In A Shallow Grave

Her Dead Body Found

129

My Dealer Helps Me

He Waits On The Street Corner

Knowing I'll Be Back

130

He Was So Not Pleased

I Couldn't Stop Laughing At Him

I Am Still John Doe

131

Darkness Surrounds Me

Enveloping Who I Am

Struggling For The Light

132

Living Life's Struggles

What Is Your Emergency

But Just Speak Slowly

133

Walking In The Park

Feeling The Gentle Air Flow

She Completes My Life

134

My Future Is Bleak

A Shotgun Pressed To My Cheek

I Cause My Own Death

135

I Sit In My Chair

I See Her Fear And Her Tears

They Put On My Hood

136

Hit The Crystal Shard

Begins To Smoke As I Toke

I'm Soaring So High

137

For All Of Her Lies

Feeling Her Life Ebb Away

Her Life She Now Lacks

A Few Extra Things

Sonnet
This is the first and only sonnet I have written:

In Shadows Deep, Where Darkness Once Did Reign,

I Wandered Lost, A Soul In Dire Dismay,

With Every Drink And Drug To Numb The Pain,

I Traded Light For Night, For Skies Of Gray.

But In The Depths, A Glimmer Shone So Bright,

A Spark Of Hope, A Whisper In The Dark,

It Called Me Forth, To Battle For The Light,

To Heal My Wounds, Ignite A Brand New Spark.

Through Trials Fierce, I Stumbled, But I Rose,

With Each New Day, A Step Towards The Dawn,

In Sober Breath, I Found A Sweet Repose,

And In My Heart, A Strength To Carry On.

Now Free From Chains, My Spirit Soars Above,

A Testament To Strength, To Life, To Love.

Spoken Word
This is something I wrote in a spoken word format. I recorded it but have yet to release it. I thought I would include it here. Hope you enjoy it.

In The Quiet Before The Storm, Before The Break Of Dawn,

There's A Whisper, A Tremor, A Soul Reborn.

Addiction, They Say, Is A Beast In The Night,

But Listen Closely—It's Also A Fight.

A Fight For The Morning We Wish To See,

A Battle With Shadows We Long To Be Free.

It Starts With A Sip, A Smoke, A Small Bet,

A Gamble With Destiny, A Dance With Regret.

It's The Allure Of The Escape, The Promise Of Bliss,

An Oasis In Deserts, A Serpent's Hiss.

We're Drawn To The Fire, Though We Know We'll Burn,

For In The Flicker Of Flames, We See A Chance To Turn.

Turn Away From The Pain, The Sorrow, The Loss,

But The Bridge We Cross Is Covered In Moss.

Slippery, Uncertain, With Each Step We Take,

We're Gambling With Pieces Of Our Soul At Stake.

Addiction Isn't Choosy, It Loves Us All The Same,

Rich Or Poor, Young Or Old, Life's Cruel Game.

It Whispers Sweet Nothings, Promises Of Power,

But Leaves Us In Ruins, A Wilted, Dying Flower.

Yet, Here's The Thing About The Night, It Always Ends,

And With The Dawn, A Message The Universe Sends.

Hope Is A Phoenix, From Ashes, It Rises,

Offering Us A Chance At New Disguises.

Recovery, A Journey, A Path Less Trod,

It's Rocky, It's Steep, But It's A Path To God.

A God Of Our Understanding, A Higher Power,

A Force That Blooms Within, A Resilient Flower.

So Let's Talk About Addiction, Not As A Chain,

But As A Chapter In Our Story, A Momentary Rain.

For After The Storm, The Air Is Clear,

And What Was Once Distant, Is Suddenly Near.

This Is Not A Solo Journey, We Walk Hand In Hand,

With Those Who've Traversed This No Man's Land.

Together, We're Stronger, A Formidable Crew,

With Love, Understanding, And Perspectives Anew.

So Here's To The Fighters, The Warriors, The Brave,

Dancing With Shadows, The Lives They Save.

Addiction, You May Have Started The War,

But We're The Authors Of This Lore.

We Write Our Endings, We Define Our Fate,

With Courage, With Kindness, We Navigate.

This Spoken Word, A Testament, A Declaration,

To The Spirit Of Survival, A Standing Ovation.

To All Those Fighting Battles Unseen,

Remember, You're A King, You're A Queen.

In The Tapestry Of Life, Every Thread Is Needed,

With Love, With Grace, We Have Succeeded.

Limerick
Here are two limericks I wrote on a whim:

1

There Once Was A Man From Dundee,

Whose Vices Were Many, You See,

He Sought In A Flask,

An Escape From The Past,

But Found Strength In Sobriety's Plea.

2

In A Town By The Shimmering Bay,

A Woman Found Darkness Each Day,

But She Fought Through The Night,

For A Future So Bright,

And Now In The Sun She Does Play.

Free Verse
I experimented with a free-verse poem. This was the result.

In The Quiet Corners Of The Night,

Where Shadows Whisper Secrets,

A Hunger Stirs, Deep And Relentless,

An Uninvited Guest,

Clinging To The Bones Like A Second Skin.

Eyes Search For Solace In The Bottom Of A Glass,

Or The Whisper Of A Flame,

A Fleeting Moment Of Escape,

Where The World Blurs,

And Pain Melts Into Nothingness.

Once, Freedom Tasted Sweet,

A Distant Memory,

Now Shackled By The Weight Of Want,

Every Breath, A Struggle,

Every Heartbeat, A Reminder.

Fingers Tremble, Reaching For The Familiar,

The Known, The Cursed Comfort,

A Dance Of Despair,

Where Hope Waltzes With Agony,

And Dreams Dissolve Into The Night.

Voices Echo In The Mind,

A Cacophony Of Guilt And Longing,

Promises Made, And Broken,

A Tapestry Of Lies,

Woven With Threads Of Regret.

Yet, In The Darkest Hours,

A Flicker, A Spark,

The Glimmer Of Something More,

A Life Not Bound By Chains,

A Soul Not Shackled By Desire.

The Road Is Long, And Winding,

Paved With Tears And Blood,

But Somewhere, Beyond The Horizon,

A Dawn Waits,

Where Light Will Pierce The Night,

And Chains Of Desire Will Fall Away,

Leaving Only The Truth Of Who We Are,

And The Strength To Be Free.

An Ode

I also wrote an Ode after reading a couple for a college class I was taking.

Oh, Addiction, Thou Art A Phantom Vile,

A Shadow Lurking In The Heart's Fragile Mile,

A Whisper In The Night, A Siren's Call,

Yet In Thy Grip, Many A Soul Doth Fall.

Thy Grip, Unyielding, Tightens Like A Chain,

Binding Minds With Pleasure, Yet Leaving Pain,

Promises Of Solace In A Fleeting Kiss,

Yet Doth Abandon, Leave Souls Amiss.

Thy Potion, Sweet, A Nectar Of Despair,

Transforms The Vibrant Soul To One Stripped Bare,

In Moments Fleeting, Joy Seems To Arise,

Yet Swiftly Fades, Leaving Empty Skies.

Oh, Dark Enchantress, Weaving Webs So Fine,

In Your Embrace, Hearts And Hopes Entwine,

The Dance Begins With Steps Of Pure Delight,

But Ends In Shadows, Far From Morning Light.

Yet In The Darkest Depths, A Spark Remains,

A Flame Of Hope Amidst Thy Cruel Reigns,

For In The Struggle, Strength Begins To Grow,

A Testament To Life's Enduring Glow.

Thou Art A Teacher, Harsh, Yet Truth Reveals,

In Brokenness, A Chance For Heart To Heal,

For Every Fall, A Rise Must Then Ensue,

In Pain, A Path To Clarity And View.

Oh, Addiction, Thou Art A Double-Edged Blade,

In Your Descent, Life's Lessons Are Displayed,

A Journey Long, Through Darkness To The Dawn,

Where Souls, Once Lost, Find Strength To Carry On.

In Overcoming Thee, The Spirit Soars,

Reclaims The Joy That Once Was Lost To Wars,

With Every Battle Fought And Victory Won,

A Testament To Life's Bright, Rising Sun.

So, Here I Sing, An Ode Both Dark And Bright,

To Thee, Addiction, Shadow Of The Night,

For In Thy Realm, The Strength Of Heart Is Found,

And In The Struggle, Life's True Colors Crowned.

Villanelle

I tried writing a Villanelle, a French-style poem, after the same college course I was taking. I had never heard of the style, and I am not positive I did it right, but here it is.

In Shadows Deep, Where Light Has Lost Its Way,

The Haunting Grip Of Vice Begins To Spread,

A Soul Confined, In Darkness Forced To Stay.

Each Fleeting High, A Fleeting Bright Array,

Deceptive Warmth Where Fear And Hope Are Wed,

In Shadows Deep, Where Light Has Lost Its Way.

A Whispered Plea For Dawn To End The Fray,

Yet Night Persists, A Void Where Dreams Have Bled,

A Soul Confined, In Darkness Forced To Stay.

Promises Break, Like Glass They Fall, Betray,

The Fragile Heart Where Silent Tears Are Shed,

In Shadows Deep, Where Light Has Lost Its Way.

Once Vibrant Hues Now Fade To Dullest Gray,

A Life Undone, By Hunger's Endless Thread,

A Soul Confined, In Darkness Forced To Stay.

Eclipsed By Need, A Life Begins To Sway,

In Endless Dark, Where Shadows' Grip Is Dread,

In Shadows Deep, Where Light Has Lost Its Way,

A Soul Confined, In Darkness Forced To Stay.

Thank You

Dear Readers,

Thank you for taking the time to read my poetry book. Your willingness to engage with my words and thoughts means the world to me. This collection is especially significant as it represents a reworking and, I hope, an improvement upon my previous efforts.

Every poem in this book has been crafted with care, reflecting my growth and evolving perspective as a poet. I am deeply grateful for your support and for allowing my work to be a part of your reading journey.

Your presence as a reader is a gift that I cherish. Thank you for your time, your attention, and your appreciation of poetry.

With heartfelt gratitude,

Brett C. Persson

8/2/2024

Other Works by Brett C. Persson

Poetry of an Addict

More Poetry of an Addict

Haikus of an Addict

Poetry of an Addict: Complete Edition

Inept & Random Thoughts Captured in Haiku

A Leaf on the Wind: A Collection of Tanka Poetry

Just A Passing Moment In Time: A Journey from Life to Death in Haiku

A Lost Soul Found in the Darkness: The Journey of a Soul in Haiku

The Ending of the Path: A Collection of Haiku

11/14/11